S0-ANQ-006

TOMORROW'S TECHNOLOGY

by Irwin Math

Morse, Marconi, and You
Wires and Watts
Bits and Pieces
More Wires and Watts
Tomorrow's Technology

TOMORROW'S TECHNOLOGY

Experimenting with the Science of the Future

IRWIN MATH

Illustrations by Hal Keith

CHARLES SCRIBNER'S SONS • NEW YORK
Maxwell Macmillan Canada • Toronto
Maxwell Macmillan International
New York • Oxford • Singapore • Sydney

Charles Scribner's Sons Books for Young Readers
Macmillan Publishing Company, 866 Third Avenue, New York, NY 10022

Maxwell Macmillan Canada, Inc.
1200 Eglinton Avenue East, Suite 200, Don Mills, Ontario M3C 3N1

Macmillan Publishing Company is part of the Maxwell Communication Group of Companies.

First edition 10 9 8 7 6 5 4 3 2 1
Printed in the United States of America

Library of Congress Cataloging-in-Publication Data
Math, Irwin.
Tomorrow's technology : experimenting with the science of the future / Irwin Math ; illustrations by Hal Keith. — 1st ed.
p. cm. Includes index.
ISBN 0-684-19294-2
1. Technology. 2. Science. I. Title.
T45.M39 1992 600—dc20 91-32341

Dla mojej Wisi

CONTENTS

LIST OF ILLUSTRATIONS

FOREWORD

Many of us today gain our "knowledge" of the future from sources such as the science-fiction films that have become so much a part of our lives. These high-budget movies, with their dazzling special effects, make spaceships, humanlike robots, matter transmitters, and laser weapons totally commonplace. So familiar are these devices that one can easily assume that they *are* the future!

This, however, is not necessarily the case. The devices of the future will be outgrowths of the technologies that exist now—just as our jet aircraft, nuclear power plants, and satellite communications systems came from developments in the first half of the twentieth century. While no one knows what paths these developments will take, an understanding of at least some of the possibilities will make the future a bit more familiar if not predictable.

It is the purpose of this book to explain, by means of practical projects, several of the technologies that may be common in the twenty-first century. Some of the ideas presented will be developed in the future, some will not. All of the projects can be carried out with easily obtainable and inexpensive materials.

It is the author's hope that this book will help readers see the future with a clearer understanding and perhaps even choose to be part of the exciting developing technologies in the professions they choose to follow.

CHAPTER 1

Breaking the Myth

When Captain James T. Kirk, of the starship *Enterprise* in the popular television series Star Trek, asks Chief Officer Scott to "beam me up, Scotty," he is using a technology that is as advanced to us as a television set would be to a caveman. Similarly, when R2D2 and C3PO, robots in the popular *Star Wars* movies of the 1980s, talk to each other, make decisions, and experience emotions, we can only wonder whether machines will ever reach such a level of sophistication.

We do not have matter transmitters, humanlike robots, or androids, nor do we routinely travel through the galaxy in our starships. We are at a point in our technological development, however, where many of the principles behind such wonders are being thought out.

Compared with the length of time man has been on the earth, human technology is fairly new. Although archaeologists have found remains of our direct ancestors that are 30,000–75,000 years old, real technology as we know it began only a couple of hundred years ago when scientists and inventors set out to seriously understand and improve the world we live in.

As the ideas and theories began to develop into practical accomplishments, the rate of progress became very rapid. In the 1890s, while Thomas Edison was struggling to develop the first practical electric light, a German scientist, Heinrich Hertz, was experimenting with electrical waves, known as hertzian waves, or electromagnetic radiation. The science textbooks of the time called these waves "interesting laboratory curiosities with no real practical applications." A few years later, Guglielmo Marconi used these same waves to send messages over increasing distances without wires—and radio was born. Until 1903, man's dream of flying like a bird was only a dream. In that year, however, two bicycle mechanics from Dayton, Ohio, flew in a crude machine they made out of canvas, wires, bicycle parts, and an old motorcycle engine. A short six years later, commercial air travel began.

By the late 1930s, radio had evolved into television, with rudimentary black-and-white pictures on a tiny, five-inch screen. Thirty years later, full-color pictures from the surface of the moon were being received by millions of television sets, in private homes, all over the world. The technology of air travel and radio signals had merged in a way that was truly dramatic!

It is by a similar outgrowth and merging of today's ideas and accomplishments that tomorrow's technology will evolve. To try to foresee the future, one must, therefore, have an understanding of some of the possibilities.

In the chapters that follow, we will examine promising accomplishments of today that may well turn out to be the foundations of future development. While we cannot make predictions of specific devices, we *will* try to understand how the basic principles work and where developments may lead.

Arthur C. Clarke, the noted science-fiction writer, summed it all up very well in a comment he made several years ago when referring to visionaries of the past. "The future is not what it used to be," he said. In that same spirit, our future will not be quite what we expect it to be, but it will also not be totally unfamiliar.

Wind: "Free" Future Power

Anyone who has tried to open an umbrella on a windy day knows the power of the wind. Bending palm trees to the ground, causing huge tidal waves, shortening a five-hour transcontinental airplane trip by an hour, the invisible power of the wind is awesome. If we could only capture some of this "free" power and put it to work for us!

Surprisingly, to some degree, mankind has and does. Large windmills have been used for hundreds of years to grind grain into flour. Ships have crossed the earth's oceans using wind alone for power, and people have even coupled windmills to generators to produce electricity on a small scale. These methods have all been partially successful, but they share one major problem: The wind is unreliable. It comes and goes only as nature decides. We cannot turn it on and off. But if wind power is so unreliable, why is it a contender as a future source of power? Is there a way to make it more reliable? The answer to these questions will be apparent as we investigate how we can use the power of the wind.

Figure 1 is a drawing of a windmill that can be easily constructed, will cost very little, and will serve as a direct example of how the power

FIGURE 1 *Experimenter's Windmill*

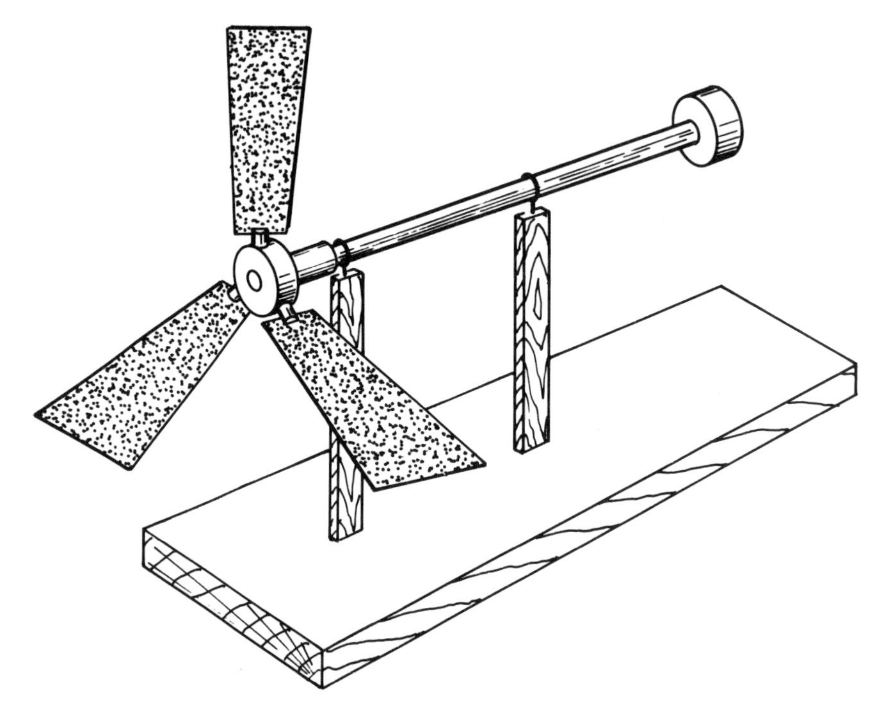

of the wind may be used. With the exception of the two screw eyes and the windmill blades, everything is made of wood—easily obtained from the scrap bin of a local lumberyard. Figure 2 shows the details of the various pieces. All of these should be constructed as carefully and accurately as possible. Use heavy cardboard, such as the back of a notepad, for the blades and give them a coat or two of shellac for strength.

When everything has been built, the windmill can be assembled. Begin by screwing the two uprights to the base with #8 by 2½-inch flat head wood screws passing through the holes in the base drilled for that purpose. Be certain that the uprights are parallel and secure. Now, carefully screw the two screw eyes to the uprights and be sure they are in line. Next, glue or press fit the windmill hub onto one end of the shaft. Slide the spacers and washers onto the shaft as shown and then

FIGURE 2 *Windmill Components*

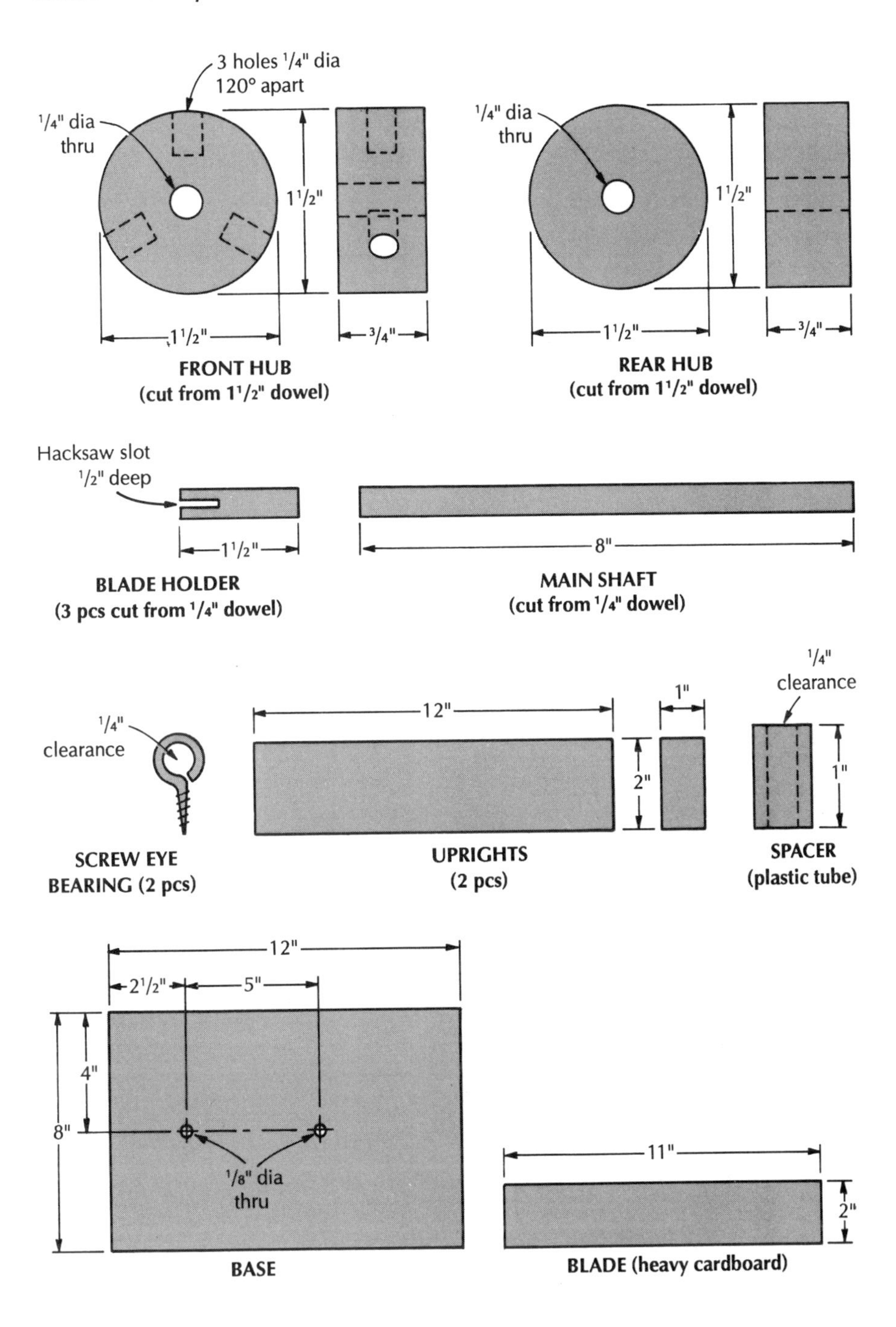

FIGURE 3 *Details of Windmill Shaft Assembly*

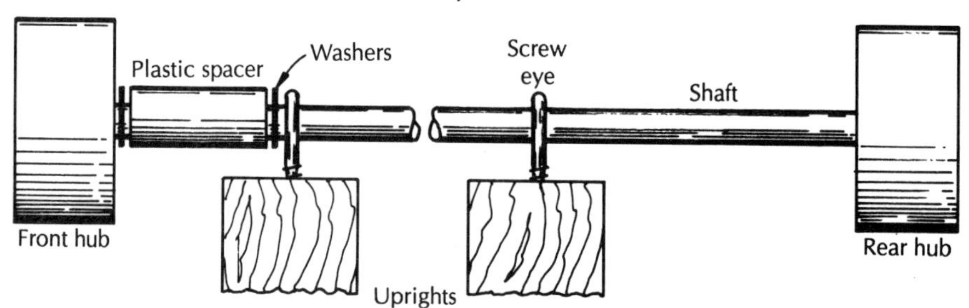

slide the whole assembly through the screw eyes. It should look like Figure 3. Readjust the angle of the screw eyes, if necessary, so that the assembly turns freely. Now, slide the three blades into the slots in the blade holders and secure them with white glue. When the glue dries, press the blade holders into the holes in the front hub and set them at a 45-degree angle as shown in Figure 4. Glue the blade holders in place. The blades should be carefully weighted by placing small bits of modeling clay at their outer ends, so that when the assembly is turned, it does not drift to any one position. Finally, liberally coat the shaft where it passes through the screw eyes with soap, petroleum jelly, or light oil.

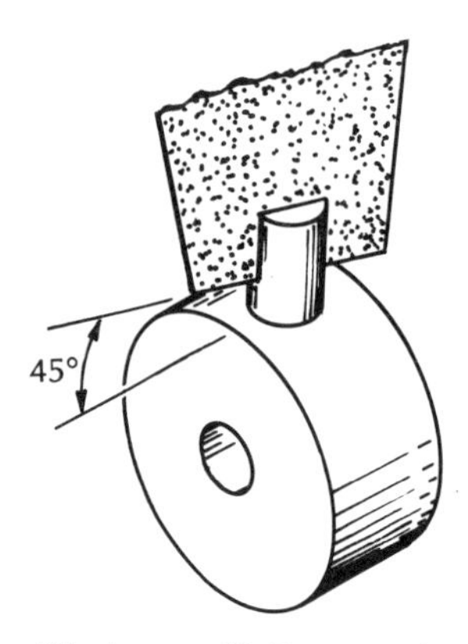

FIGURE 4 *Blades at 45-Degree Angle from Hub*

FIGURE 5 *Converting the Rear Hub to a Pulley*

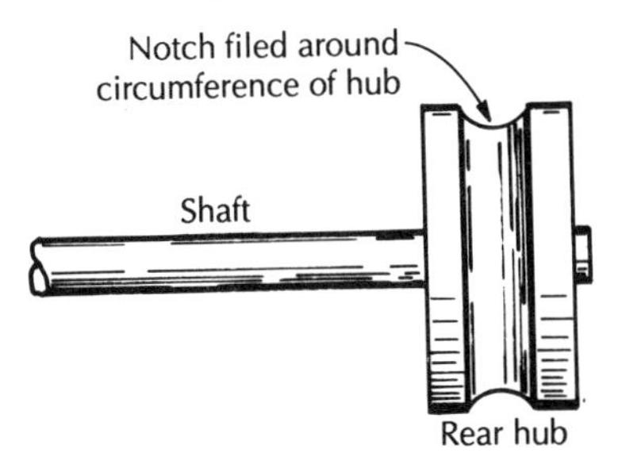

If everything has been built and assembled correctly, the windmill will turn as long as it is facing into the slightest breeze and its speed will be a function of the strength of the breeze. Now, let us put it to work generating electricity. To do this will require a little more work and the purchase of a generator and a volt-ohm-milliampere(VOM)-type meter to measure energy produced.

The generator will be a small unit of the type commonly used to provide power for a bicycle's lights. This device can usually be purchased from a local bicycle-repair shop for less than $10 if new, or for $2 or $3 if used. The only concern is that it be able to turn freely without binding. The VOM voltmeter can be any moving-pointer type that can measure at least 10 volts and 50–100 milliamperes. Digital voltmeters will work but will not give as clear an indication of variations in voltage versus speed. A suitable meter can usually be obtained from an electronics parts store for less than $10.

Figure 5 shows how to convert the rear hub into a pulley and how to attach it to the windmill shaft. Figure 6 shows how to mount the generator and, then, couple it to the pulley. The rubber-band drive belt should be long enough to fit easily over the rear hub and motor pulley and loose enough so that everything turns freely but not so loose that the drive belt slips.

If you now connect the VOM, set to volts, to the generator and place the windmill in an adequate breeze, you will see that voltage is

FIGURE 6 *How to Add a Generator to the Windmill*

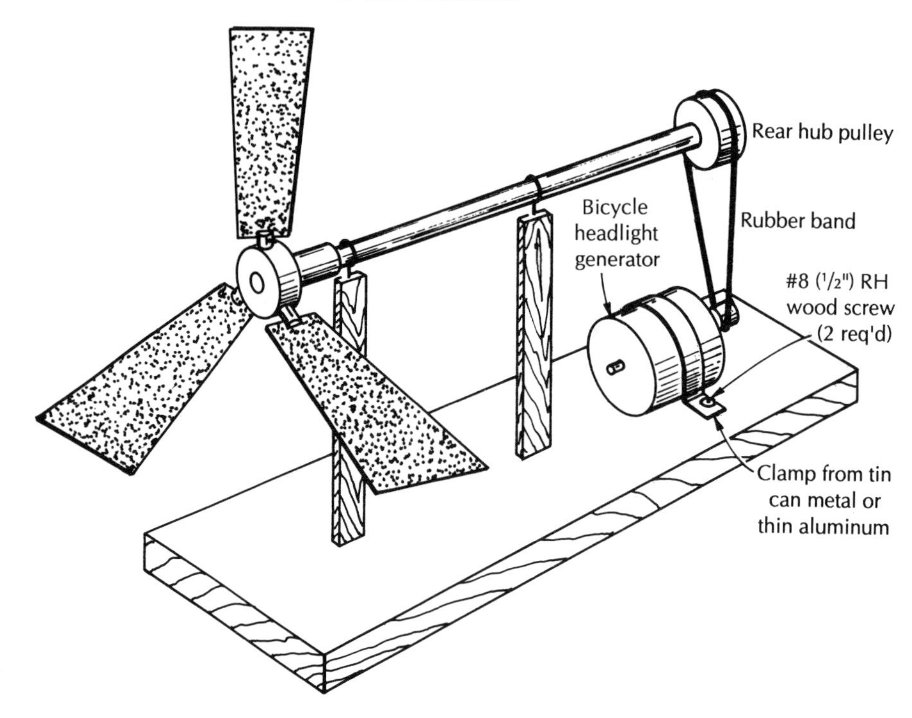

produced as it turns. The amount of voltage produced, however, will be directly proportional to the speed of the windmill. To make such a system a practical source of power requires that two problems be overcome. The first is keeping the voltage steady, or constant, and the second, maintaining the power supply independent of the presence, or absence, of wind. These problems are easier to solve than might be apparent, thanks to modern technology.

Figure 7 shows how to add a solid state regulator to the windmill. All components are readily available at a local electronics parts store for under $10. The regulator circuit will accept any input voltage from 2 to 20 volts, but will only produce an output voltage of 1.5 volts. This means that, once the windmill turns faster than a preselected minimum speed, no more than 1.5 volts will be delivered to any circuit connected

FIGURE 7 *Solid State Regulator*

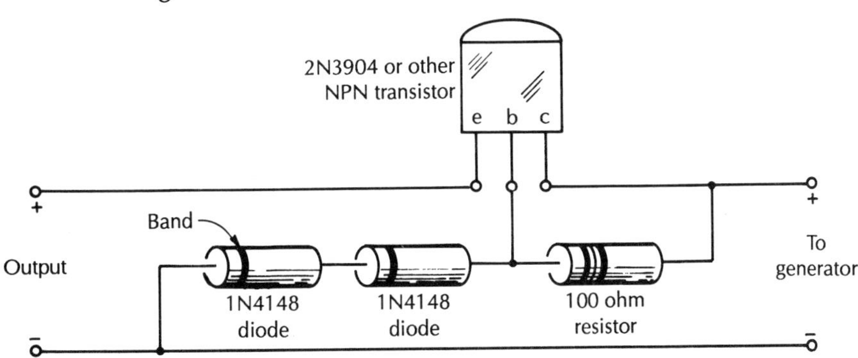

to it—no matter how much faster it turns. You can easily prove this by connecting the meter to the output of the regulator and spinning the windmill. The first problem is now solved. Figure 8 shows the solution to the second problem. The output of the regulator is, simply, connected to a rechargeable battery with one additional component to prevent overcharging. As long as the wind blows, the windmill will supply power and charge the battery. When the wind stops, power will be supplied by the battery alone—the outside world will never know anything has happened. If you now connect a flashlight bulb to the positive and negative outputs (across the battery), you will have a good demonstration

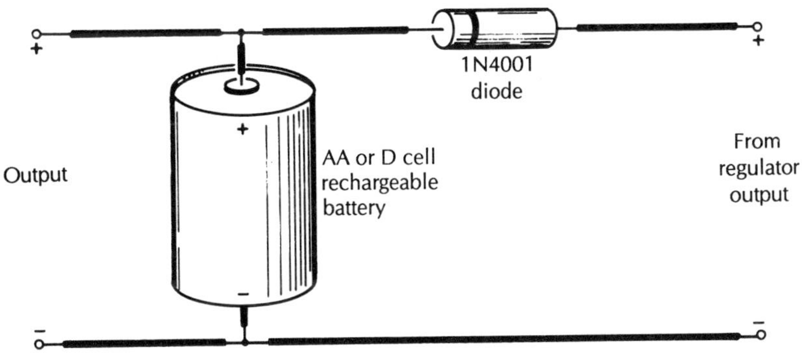

FIGURE 8 *Battery Connection*

of the entire operation of the windmill generating system. As long as the wind blows often enough to keep the battery charged, the bulb will light continuously without any noticeable dimming. In a real situation, the generator, battery, and regulator would be chosen to achieve the best compromise between the power required and the average wind speed at a particular location. Since wind power is free, uses no fuel of any kind, and is environmentally safe, it is no wonder that, in the future, one might see vast fields of modern windmills supplying a portion of our electrical requirements.

More "Free" Future Power—Solar

Getting into a car that has been parked in the sun for some length of time in warm weather is an experience that clearly demonstrates the power contained in sunlight. The interior of such a car can reach 100 degrees or more, especially in the summer. Many kinds of plastic items left on car seats are often found melted. This buildup of heat in a closed but even partially transparent (to light) enclosure is called the greenhouse effect and is the basis of a twenty-first-century energy source that is beginning to be employed today.

It has been said that 1,000 watts of energy, equivalent to the light of ten 100-watt light bulbs, is contained in every square meter of sunlight on a summer day. It is no wonder, therefore, that scientists are continually trying to find efficient ways to capture more of this "free" energy. Let's do a simple experiment to look at one way that this greenhouse effect can be put to work.

Figure 9 is a drawing of a simple wood-and-glass frame that can easily be constructed with scrap materials from a local lumberyard. Figure 10 shows the details of the various individual pieces. The glass

FIGURE 9 *Wood and Glass Greenhouse-Effect Frame*

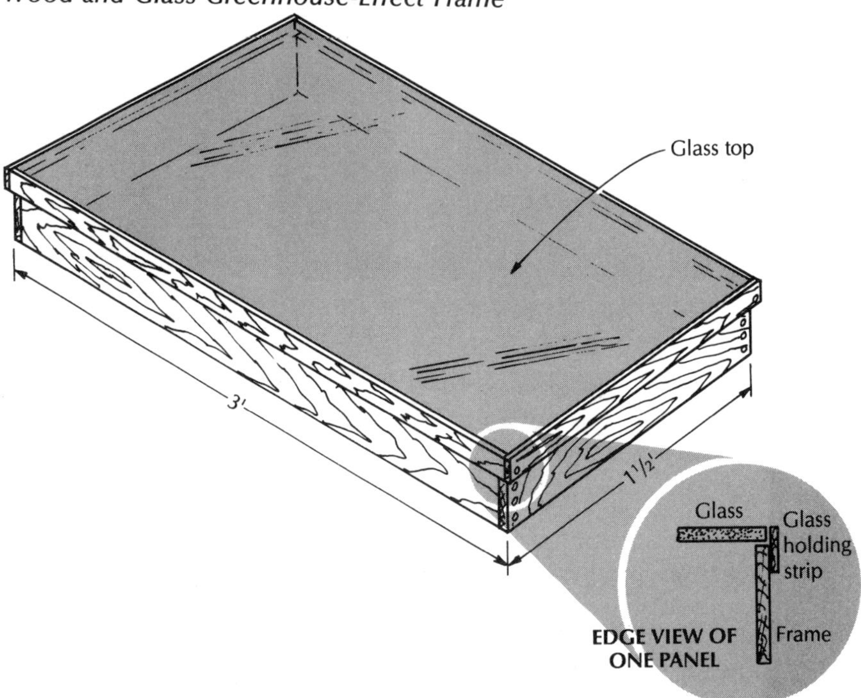

can be common window glass but should be handled with extreme caution. In fact, whenever handling glass, it is a good idea to wear a pair of work gloves for safety. Be sure to fabricate all pieces accurately and then carefully assemble the frame, using common nails for the frame and wire brads or tacks for the lattice material. Next, give all of the interior surfaces two coats of flat, black paint—allowing the first coat to completely dry before applying the second coat. Now let us see what this solar collector can do.

Move the frame to an area where sunlight can fully illuminate the black surfaces. This can be either indoors or outdoors but must be in direct sun. Obtain a thermometer such as the weather type people mount outside windows and note the temperature outside the wooden frame. Now place the thermometer in the center of the frame and carefully lower the glass cover between the lattice supports. Do not try

FIGURE 10 *Frame Components*

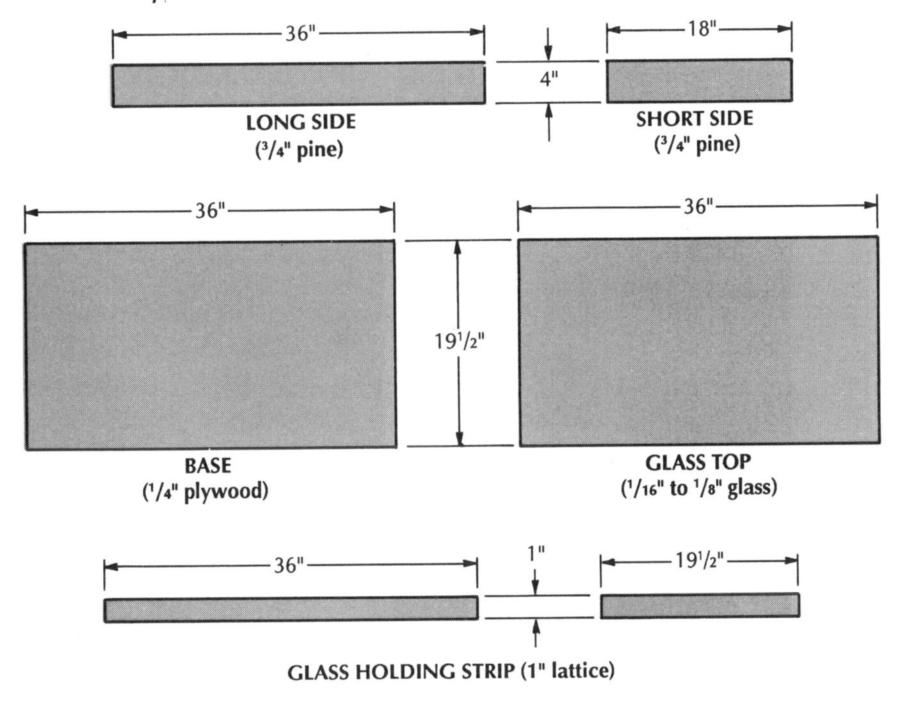

to secure the glass in place at this time; just simply lay it in position. After thirty minutes in the sun, check the temperature inside the box. It should have risen by at least fifteen to twenty degrees. It is this increase that will be used to perform a practical function: the heating of water.

Carefully remove the glass and set it aside. From a hardware store or plumbing supply shop, obtain a 6-foot length of soft, ½- or ¾-inch diameter copper tubing and six matching clamps. Very carefully form the copper tubing into the zigzag heat exchanger shown in Figure 11. Do not bend the tubing sharply or the walls will collapse. Rather, bend it slowly, a little bit at a time, around a broom handle or similar curved surface, so that the tubing remains round. You might wish to tightly fill the tubing with common beach sand to give it somewhat more rigidity while bending. The completed tubing should now be cleaned of any

FIGURE 11 *Construction of Heat Exchanger*

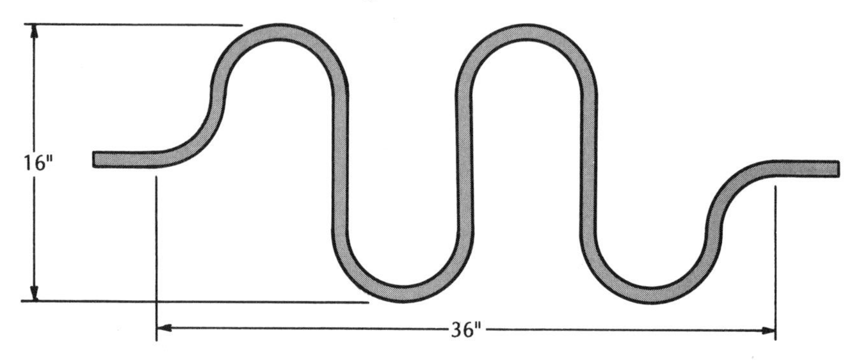

sand and mounted to the bottom of the frame with the clamps and some #8 by ½-inch round head wood screws. You should also drill two 1-inch diameter holes in the ends of the frame, as shown in Figure 12, for access to the ends of the tubing. When the heat exchanger is in position, give the copper tubing two coats of the same flat black paint you used on the inside of the frame and allow it to thoroughly dry. Carefully

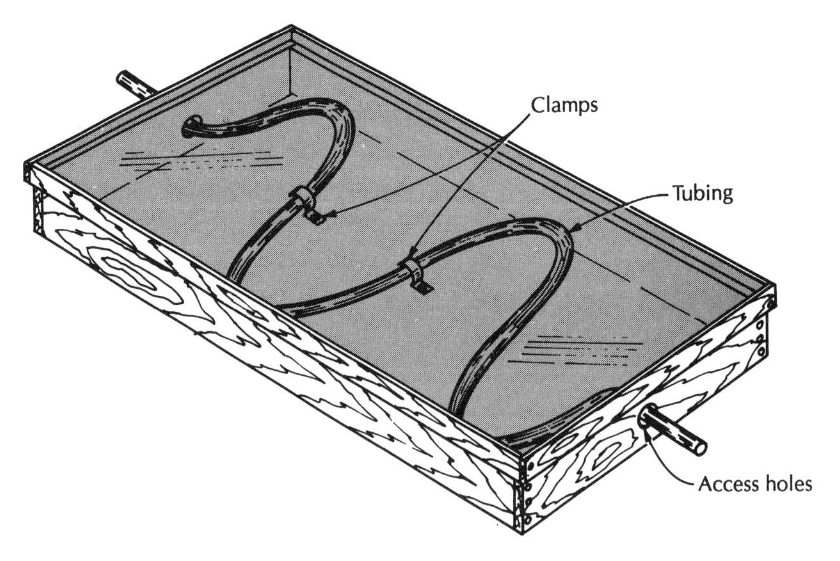

FIGURE 12 *Mounting Heat Exchanger in Frame*

FIGURE 13 *Solar Water Heater*

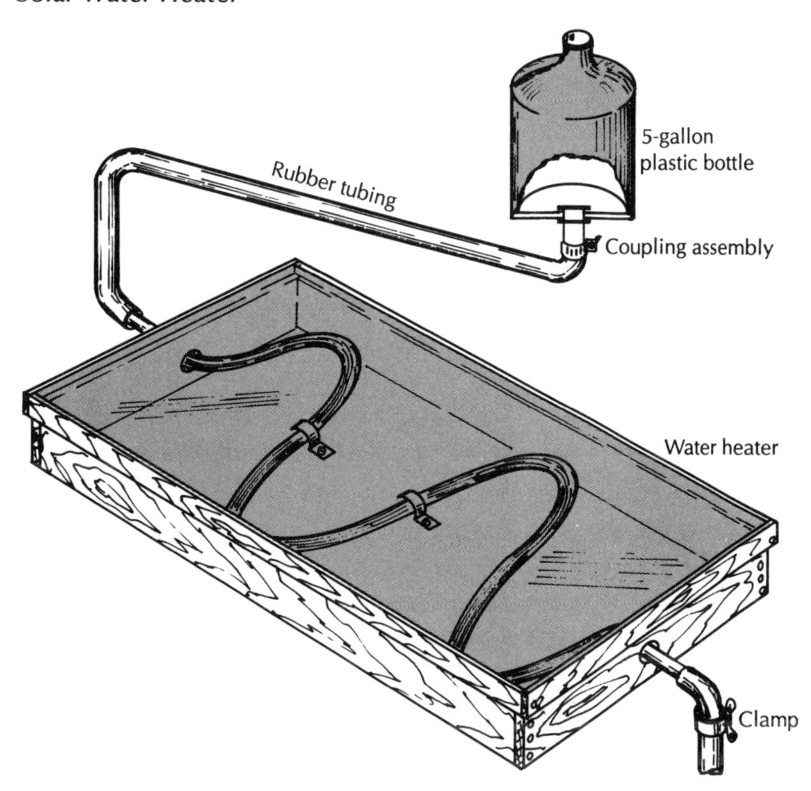

replace the glass cover, and this time secure it in place with caulking compound or silicone bathtub sealer. Be very careful that you do not break the glass. This completes the construction of the main portion of the solar collector. Now let us see how we can put it to use.

Figure 13 is a diagram of a solar water-heating system that will demonstrate a practical use of sunlight. The water supply is a 1- to 5-gallon plastic bottle with a short, copper, threaded nipple of the same size as the tubing used in the collector. The nipple is inserted into the plastic bottle by first drilling a slightly undersized hole in the bottom of the bottle. A nut, rubber washer, and flat washer are then threaded onto the nipple and the entire assembly is forced into the hole. Finally, the

FIGURE 14 *Details of Coupling*

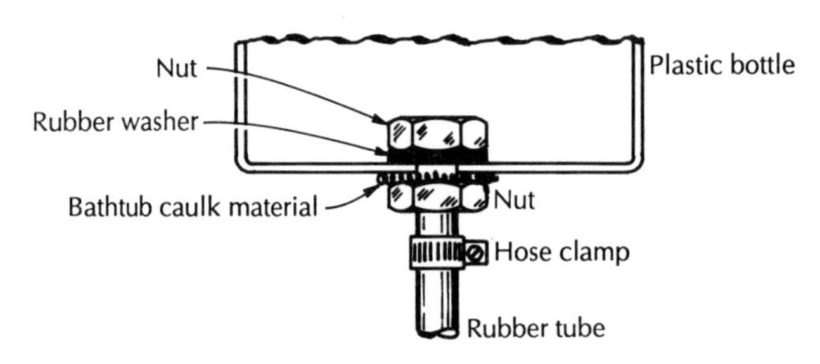

assembled unit is secured with bathtub sealer. Figure 14 shows the details of this entire procedure. When you are finished, be certain the joint is tight and doesn't leak. Now connect the tank (plastic bottle) to the input of the solar collector with a short length of rubber or plastic tubing. Slide the tubing onto the outside of the copper tubing at the collector and onto the nipple at the tank. Connect another short length of rubber or plastic tubing to the output of the collector and attach a small clamp over the end of this tube to serve as a valve.

At this point, you can bring the entire assembly outdoors and fill the tank with water. After ten to fifteen minutes in the sun, open the clamp so that the water slowly trickles out. You should be able to produce a stream of fairly hot water with this arrangement, even in cold weather.

Commercially manufactured solar heating systems based on this exact principle are being used today throughout the world to supplement gas, oil, and electric heating systems. They are, of course, much larger and more efficient than this model. They work so well in certain climates, they pay for themselves in fuel savings in a very short time. Their only drawback is that they do not work well in inclement weather. The energy they use is free and nonpolluting, however, and, eventually, scientists will discover ways of dealing even with the weather shortcoming.

Light Beam Communications and Fiber Optics

Alexander Graham Bell, the inventor of the telephone, had a plan back in 1880 to utilize sunlight in a way that is quite different from our discussion of the previous chapter. Concerned with ways to send the human voice over long distances, he realized that light would be a perfect medium for such transmissions if a way could be found to enable it to carry intelligence. After considerable thought and effort, Bell developed the device shown in Figure 15, which he called the Photophone. In operation, a mirror mounted to a thin, tightly stretched canvas diaphragm was arranged so that a beam of sunlight would strike it and be reflected to a distant listening post. When someone spoke directly into the diaphragm, it would vibrate, in accordance with the person's voice, in the same way that the sides of a thin, closed box with a small opening on one end vibrates if someone talks into it. These vibrations caused the mirror to move, which in turn caused the reflected sunbeam to also vary. At the receiving end, Bell arranged a photoelectric

FIGURE 15 *Bell's Photophone*

cell, battery, and earphones. The photoelectric cell, a device that varies the amount of electric current flowing through it as a function of the amount of light striking it, was oriented so that it was directly in the path of the modulated sunbeam. The result was clear, completely recognizable sound—even over distances of a few hundred feet.

The Photophone did not become a commercial success, since the overall mechanical stability of the system was poor and the need for sunlight made it very impractical. The idea of using modulated light to carry information was not forgotten, but not much was done until 1960 when Theodore Maiman of Hughes Research Laboratories demonstrated a source of light that was ideal for optical communications—the laser. This device produced a thin, powerful beam of light that could be directed at distant points at will. Furthermore, there was no appreciable spreading of the beam over distances of thousands of feet. Recognizing these features, scientists were quick to develop ways to use the laser to carry the human voice, as well as data communications signals—both through the air and through thin fibers made of glass, as we will see shortly.

To investigate light-beam transmissions, we can build a modern day version of Bell's Photophone using easy-to-obtain materials. Figure 16 shows the complete unit, while Figure 17 shows the individual transmitter components. The flashlight chosen should produce as thin a

FIGURE 16 *Modern Day Version of the Photophone*

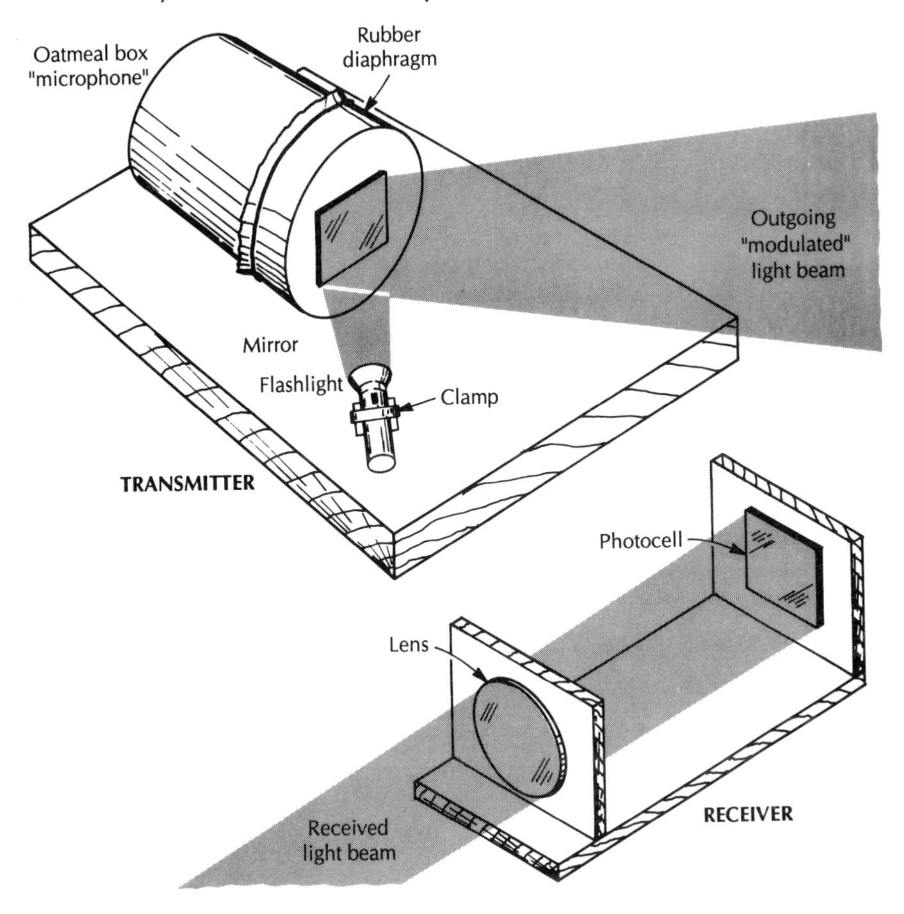

beam of light as one can find. The rest of the material is obtainable from a local lumberyard.

Start construction by building the base and flashlight cradle. Next, remove the top and bottom of a common oatmeal box. Carefully cut out a diaphragm from a toy rubber balloon and attach it to one end of the oatmeal box with a rubber band. Be certain that the rubber diaphragm is tight and evenly stretched. The diaphragm is operating properly when you can feel a slight vibration at its center while talking into the open

FIGURE 17 *Transmitter Components*

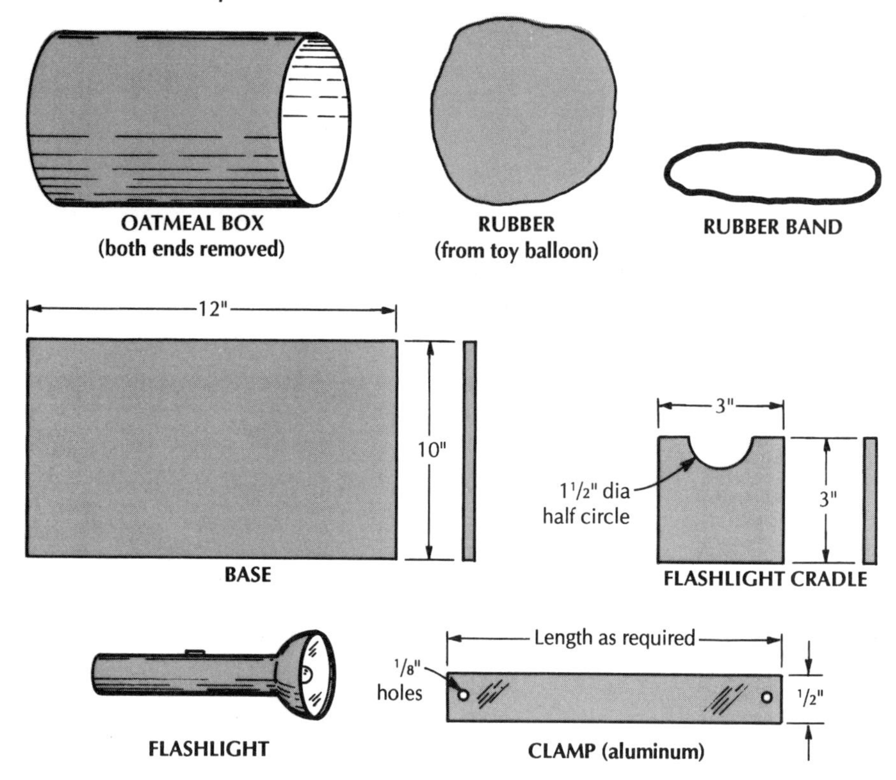

end of the oatmeal box. The oatmeal box "microphone" should be mounted to the base with #8 1-inch round head wood screws and flat washers. A very small mirror, or piece of a mirror, should be glued to the exact center of the diaphragm. Use white glue for this operation. Model airplane cement and similar solvent-based glues cannot be used because they may dissolve the rubber. Finally, arrange the flashlight in its cradle so that when switched on, it produces a beam of light, when reflected by the mirror, that is parallel to the assembly.

The receiver can now be built. Figure 18 shows its components. It is simpler than the transmitter and requires no special care other than the spacing of the lens-to-photocell distance. The photocell is a common, inexpensive, silicon solar cell, readily available at an electronics parts store. Be sure to obtain one that is at least ¼-inch square. For best

FIGURE 18 *Receiver Components*

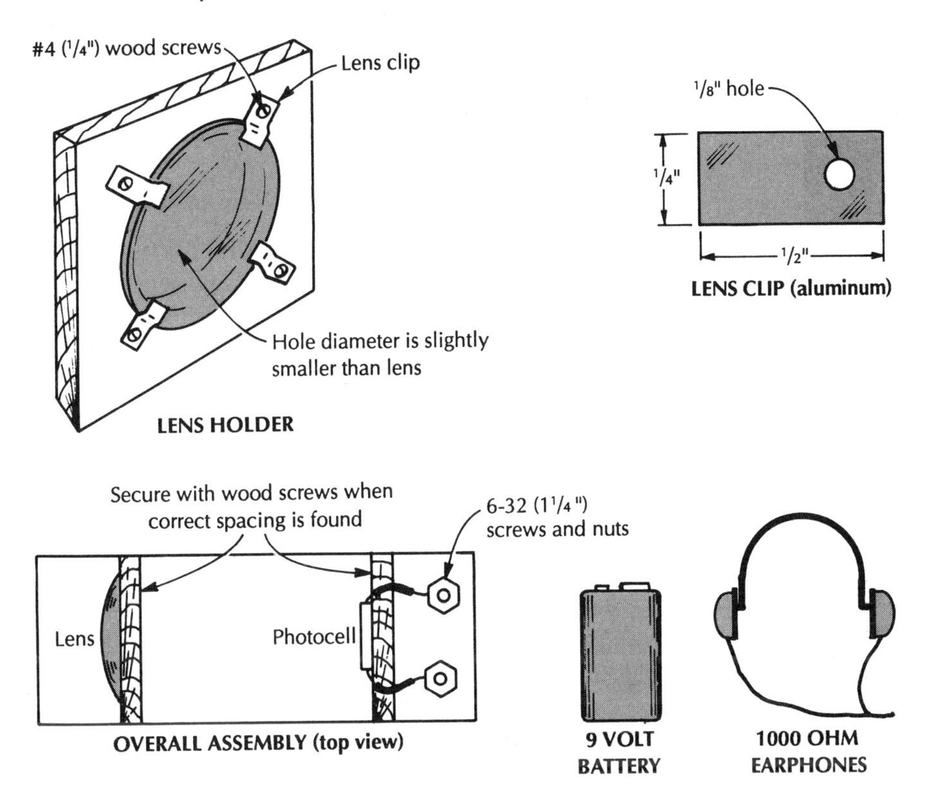

results, the earphones should be of the magnetic, high impedance type, at least 1,000 ohms. The lens can be any common, inexpensive magnifying glass that is 2 inches, or larger, in diameter.

When you have built and assembled all of the parts, arrange the receiver so that the light beam from the transmitter shines directly onto the photocell as shown in Figure 19. Place the lens in front of the photocell and slowly move it back and forth along the beam until the smallest spot of light is produced on the surface of the photocell. Secure the lens in this position. For best results, try to have the transmitter at least 25 feet away from the receiver.

To test the Photophone, connect the battery and earphone as shown in Figure 20 and, while a friend talks into the transmitter, slightly move

FIGURE 19 *Setup for Aligning Receiver Lens*

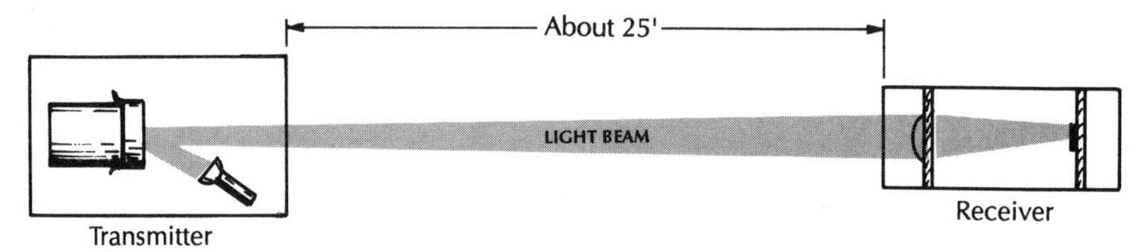

the receiver until the best overall signal is received. If you have been careful, you should be able to transmit a clear voice signal over many hundreds of feet, especially at night.

Free-space optical communication systems, applying similar principles, are in use today, employing lasers and much more sophisticated modulation methods. These systems not only carry voice but, also, video and data signals of all kinds. They have the same problem as the original Photophone, however: They are limited to a direct path between transmitter and receiver. Any obstruction or inclement weather can interfere with their signals.

A light-beam communications technology that does not have these disadvantages is called fiber optics. This technology utilizes the same principles of the free-space systems, except that the modulated light is carried through hair-thin fibers made of ultrapure glass. So pure is this glass, that the light can travel many miles before it becomes too weak to detect.

Figure 21 shows how an optical fiber works. The fiber consists of a central core and outer jacket, or cladding, each made of a different type of glass. The two glasses are selected so that a light beam entering the core is constantly reflected from the outer cladding back into the

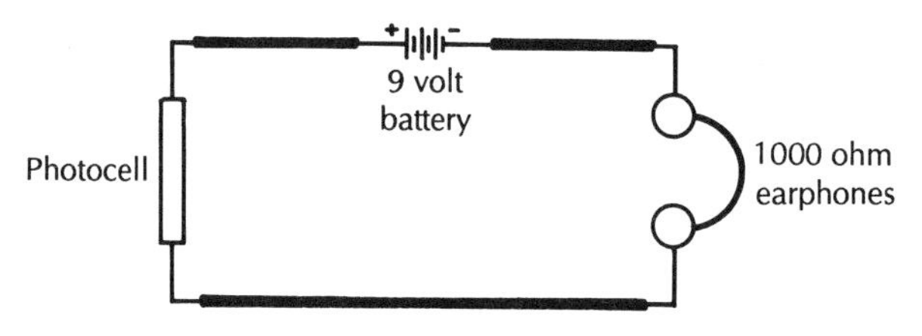

FIGURE 20 *Wiring Diagram of Receiver*

FIGURE 21 *Operation of an Optical Fiber*

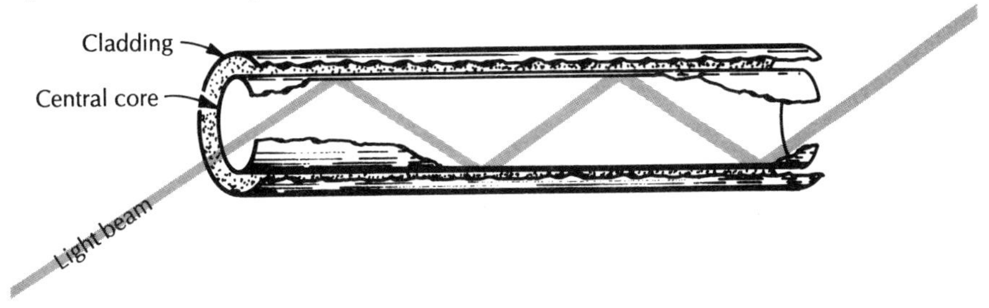

core until it finally exits at the far end. As a result, light is trapped within the fiber and will travel around corners and through angles in the same way that an electrical current travels in a copper wire.

Figure 22 is a photograph of a typical commercial fiber-optic transmitter and receiver. An optical transmitter first converts an electrical signal into modulated light and "launches" this light into an optical fiber. The fiber conducts the light to a distant point where an optical receiver then converts the modulated light from the fiber back into a replica of the original electrical signal. Figure 23 shows the construction details of a typical fiber-optic cable.

To fully appreciate the benefits of a fiber-optic transmission system,

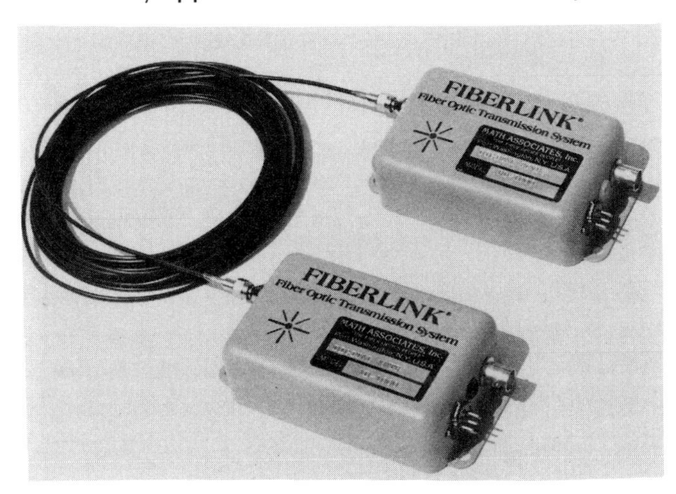

FIGURE 22 *Typical Fiber-Optic Transmission System*

FIGURE 23 *Construction Details of a Fiber-Optic Cable*

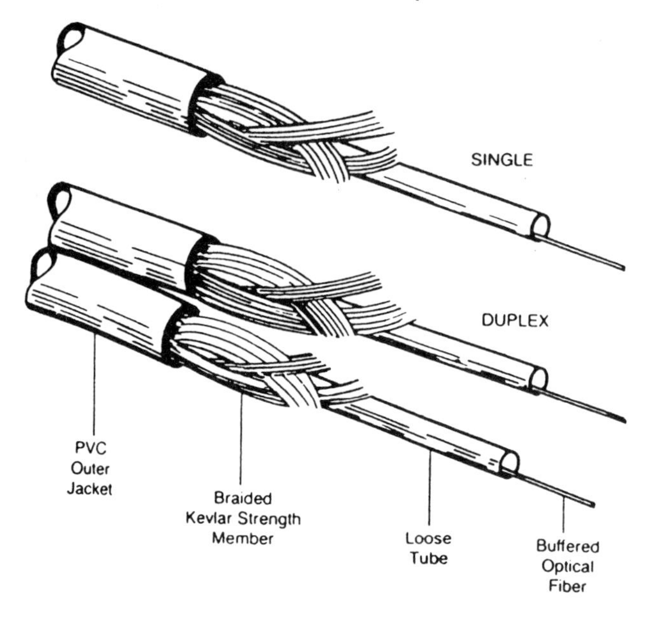

it is important to remember two basic facts: the optical fiber is made of glass, and the signal carrier is light. There is no electrical path or metallic connection between the two ends of the system. Since the carrier is light, external electrical signals have no effect on the transmission. Stray radio frequency energy, high voltage power lines, and even lightning will not cause a ripple of static. The signal is virtually interference free. Also, since the fiber is made of glass, it is unaffected by most chemicals or solvents. A fiber-optic cable can be used in chemical plants as well as in oil and gas refineries. A broken fiber will neither cause a spark leading to an explosion, nor will it create a hazardous condition to personnel. In addition, since there is no electrical current, the effects of water are nonexistent. Short circuits simply do not occur. As a result of these advantages, fiber-optic transmission systems account for more than 80 percent of long distance telephone transmissions in the United States today. Fiber optics have many other critical industrial applications. By the twenty-first century, this technology will be as common as copper-wire technology was in the twentieth century.

CHAPTER 5

Electro-Optical Detection and Recognition

We are all familiar with the laser scanners that read prices at the local supermarket or those that quickly and accurately identify valid dollar bills in money-changing machines. They sometimes seem to do their simple tasks much better than a person ever could. As clever as these devices are, however, reading devices of the future will do much more. Not only will they read numbers and text, they will instantly recognize common objects and even people. Enough of the basic principles of this twenty-first-century technology are in use today to almost assure these uses of scanners.

We see things as the result of patterns of light falling on sensitive cells in the retinas of our eyes. Our brain then takes these patterns, in the form of nerve impulses, and processes them so that we can quickly identify objects we have previously learned to recognize. A similar function can be performed electronically. Figure 24 shows an instrument for recognizing a penny, nickel, dime, or quarter that can easily be constructed. Although it is far simpler than a true image-recognition system, it does use some of the same basic principles.

FIGURE 24 *Coin Recognizer*

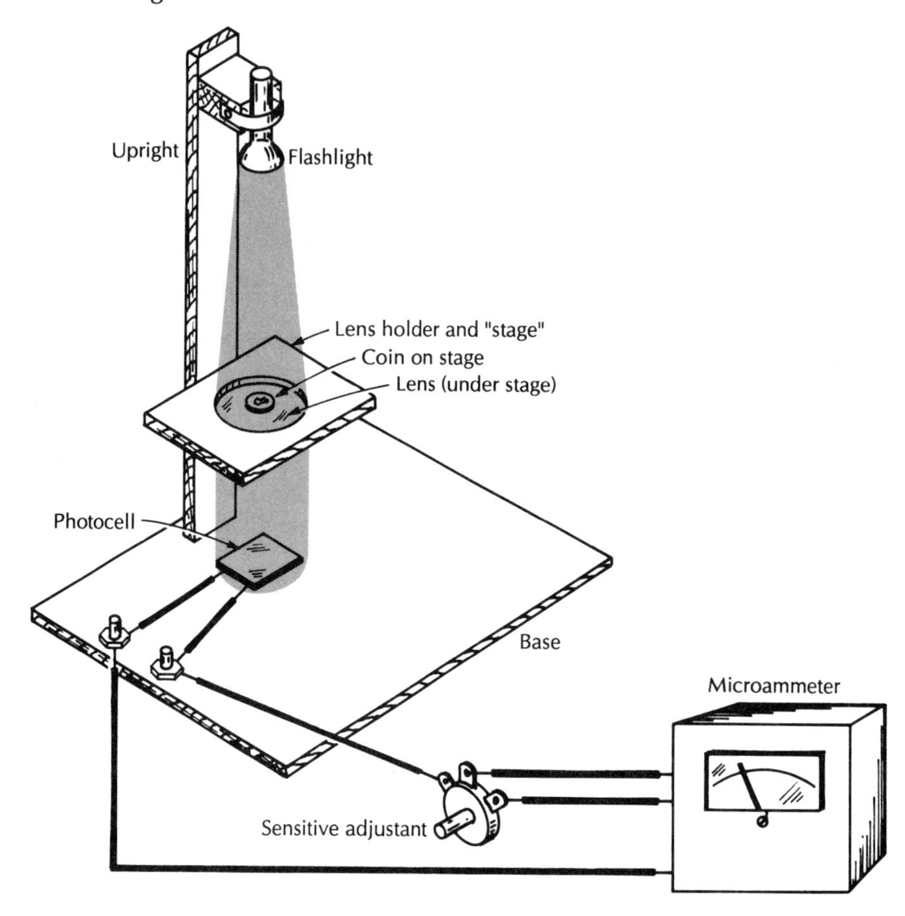

As can be seen from the diagram, a beam of light from a flashlight is directed so that it fully illuminates a small opening on a "stage" where the object to be identified will be placed. A lens is then located underneath the stage and adjusted so that all of the light passing through the opening in the stage is focused on a photocell. The photocell is, in turn, connected to a sensitive meter, which then indicates how much light is reaching the photocell and, as a result, shows which coin has been placed on the stage.

Start construction by building all of the parts shown in Figure 25. The photocell, lens, and flashlight are the same as the ones used in the Photophone in the last chapter. The meter can be your VOM, or, for a

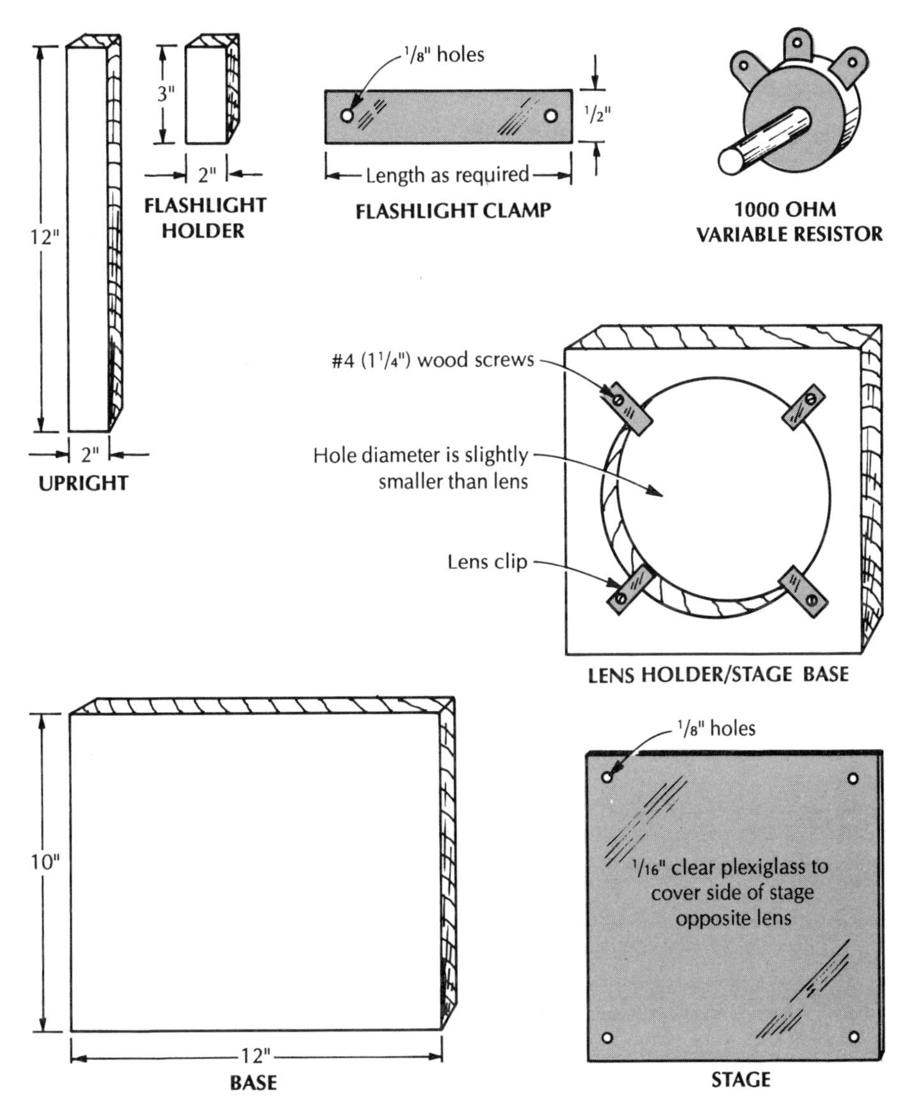

FIGURE 25 *Coin Recognizer Components*

complete, self-contained project, it can be an inexpensive panel meter with a full-scale range of up to 1 to 10 milliamperes. Most electronic parts suppliers will have suitable units for a few dollars. You can obtain the 1,000 ohm variable resistor from this source as well.

Make all the parts carefully and assemble everything except the lens holder/stage as shown. If you use an empty aluminum soda can as a source of material for the flashlight clamp, you can use a pair of heavy scissors to cut out the strip. Do not connect the meter to the photocell yet. First, turn on the flashlight and adjust its orientation so that the area where the stage will be is fully illuminated. Next, adjust the spacing of the lens holder so that the smallest spot of light possible falls on the surface of the photocell and is centered on it. This adjustment is very important and will determine the overall accuracy of the unit.

When you have succeeded in properly aligning the lens and photocell, permanently mount the lens holder in position on the upright. Now, connect the meter and variable resistor as shown in Figure 26. The variable resistor should then be adjusted so that the meter just rests on the full-scale reading with nothing on the stage. Finally, with a grease pencil or thin strips of adhesive tape, outline a small box in the center of the stage to locate the position for the unknown coin. It is now time to calibrate the recognition system.

Place a dime on the center of the stage and note the meter reading. This point will be called 10 cents. Repeat with a penny, nickel, and

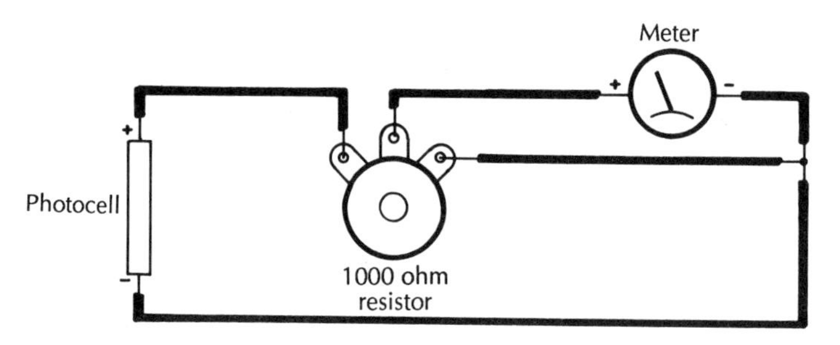

FIGURE 26 *Wiring of Coin Recognizer*

quarter. You will note that each coin allows a different amount of light to pass and, therefore, gives a different meter reading. By referring to the meter readings alone, you can easily determine the value of the coin on the stage. In the case of a commercial coin-reader, a computer would interpret these readings while the coin was in motion. It could then control the amount of change to be given, or perform some other function, in a fraction of a second. It might also weigh the coin or check on its magnetic properties to further determine if it was real or a counterfeit.

Our coin reader, as we have just seen, operates by measuring the amount of light that passes between a coin and a fixed opening. Its principle is not limited to coins, however. If the light source is very stable in brightness, and the meter is calibrated very carefully with objects of a known physical size and shape, the device is capable of high accuracy—as long as only those specific objects are placed upon its stage. But what about objects that are the same size and shape, such as the dollar bills we spoke about at the beginning of this chapter? How can an electro-optical circuit recognize them?

Figure 27 shows the top view of a rearrangement of the components

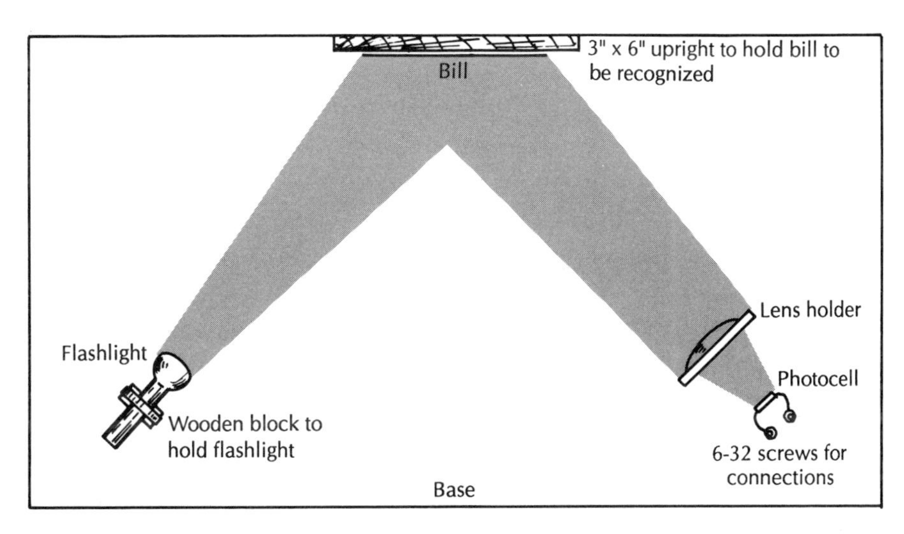

FIGURE 27 *Top View of Rearranged Components for Surface Recognizer*

of the coin reader. Now light from the flashlight illuminates the surface of the object and the lens/photocell combination measures the reflected light. The meter doesn't know where the light is coming from—it only measures the amount of light on the photocell. The result, however, is exactly the same. Dollar bills reflect slightly different amounts of light than 5-dollar bills, 10-dollar bills, or scraps of paper, for that matter. At some level most objects, even similar ones, have their own distinctive reflective signature. If you were to now imagine combining a surface reader with a shape reader, some clever electronics, and, perhaps, a computer program designed specifically for the purpose, you could begin to understand how more sophisticated recognition systems can be built. With the size of computer chips shrinking and their complexity expanding, there is virtually no limit to the types of recognition systems that will be built tomorrow.

Robotics

The robots portrayed in the popular, science-fiction movies and television programs all seem to be quite human. They react to their surroundings, make decisions, and, often, seem to be so much more intelligent than their human counterparts that one wonders if such thinking machines will ever be produced by man. The technology required to produce a truly artificial person simply does not exist today. What does exist, however, are mechanisms, principles, and concepts that may someday lead to the development of humanlike robots. In the previous chapter we have already seen how a simple object-recognition system could be implemented.

To further explore the basic concept of how a robot of the future might be built, we will examine two current approaches to the imitation of human functions. Figure 28 is a circuit that is probably familiar to all of us, costs very little to implement, and clearly demonstrates how a mechanism can respond to its surroundings. The circuit will require a thermostat, a small battery-operated fan, and two D cell batteries. The thermostat is the type commonly used to control the heat produced by oil or gas burners in our homes. Heating unit contractors or repair shops

FIGURE 28 *Simple Heat-Sensing Circuit*

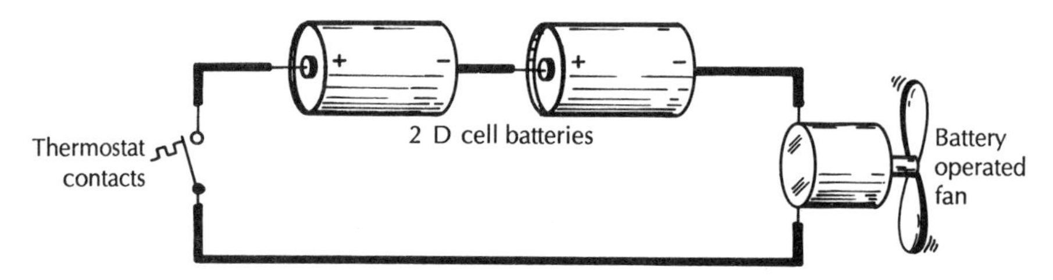

will often be glad to donate one of the older types since many of these are being replaced by newer, computer-chip-controlled units. Be certain that the one you get is in operating order and that it is one of the simplest types. The round Honeywell, or equivalent, shown in Figure 29 is the best. When you obtain a suitable thermostat, remove the round cover by gently pulling it off its mounting clips. Hold the unit level, vertically (the way it would be mounted to a wall), and, while moving the dial above and below room temperature, locate the terminals that connect to the switch mechanism. On some thermostats these will be mechanical contacts; on others, a small, glass envelope containing a drop of mercury and some wire contacts will be used. In either case, set the unit 10

FIGURE 29 *Suitable Thermostat for Environmental Response Experiment*

FIGURE 30 *Internal Details of Thermostat Switches*

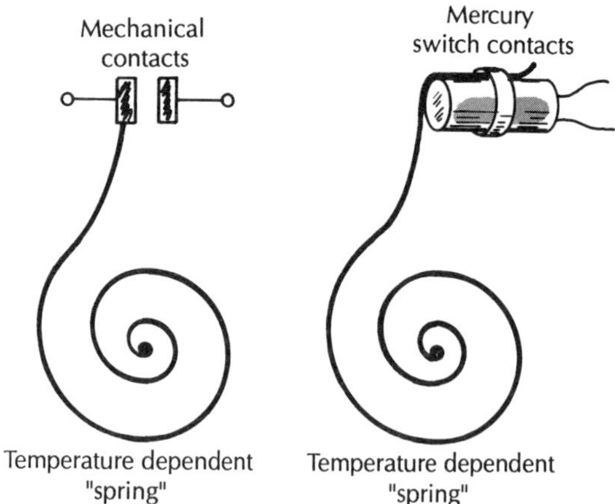

degrees or more below room temperature, and identify the terminals that connect to the open, or nonconducting, switch contacts. On the simplest thermostats, these will be the only switch contacts. On the more complicated ones, there may be an additional, normally closed, or conducting, set of contacts. These are unnecessary for our purposes. Figure 30 shows the internal details of two types of thermostats suitable for this experiment.

The fan required for this project may be purchased, or it may be made from an inexpensive motor and plastic blades. Fans of the type needed may be readily obtained from gadget outlets for a dollar or so. If you cannot find a suitable fan, obtain a small, inexpensive DC motor from a local electronics parts supplier. You will also need a matching fan blade. If you purchase the complete fan, you will need a way to electrically turn the unit on and off without using the fan's internal switch. Figure 31 shows how to accomplish this. The cardboard disk

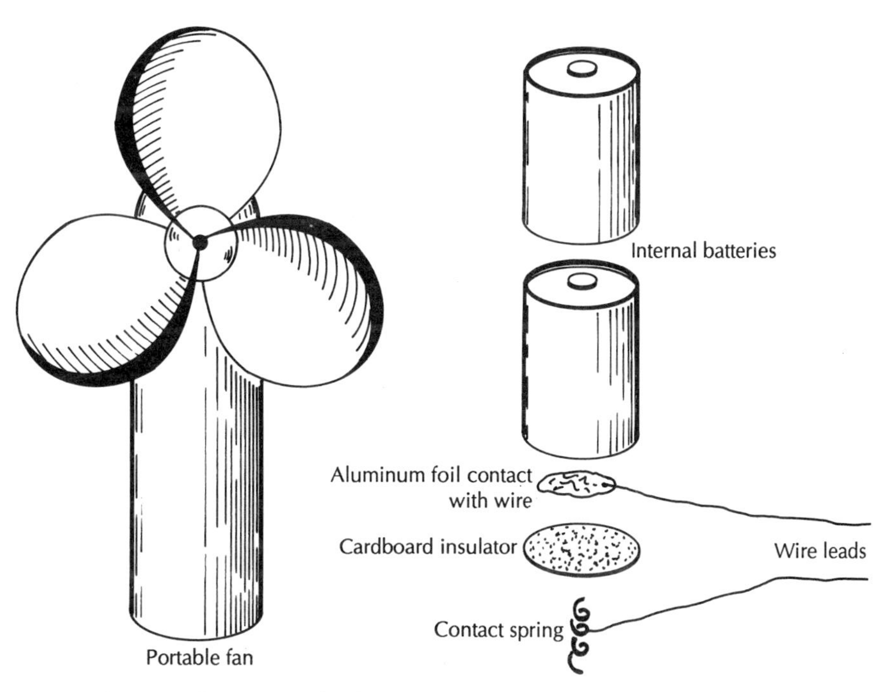

FIGURE 31 *External Wires for Control of Portable Fan*

prevents the circuit to the fan's motor from being completed until two external wires are connected together. The wires should be routed through a small opening made in the fan housing for that purpose.

When everything is prepared, make certain that the fan goes on and off as the wires are connected and disconnected. Now, build the parts shown in Figure 32. Assemble the base and, then, support and mount the fan and thermostat facing each other as shown in Figure 33. If the thermostat is the kind with a mercury-type switch, be certain it is absolutely level. Next, connect all components as shown—then, check that setting the thermostat higher than room temperature turns the fan on and setting it lower turns the fan off. Finally, set the thermostat as close as possible to the reading where the fan just about comes on.

Now, let us examine what we have built. The thermostat senses the

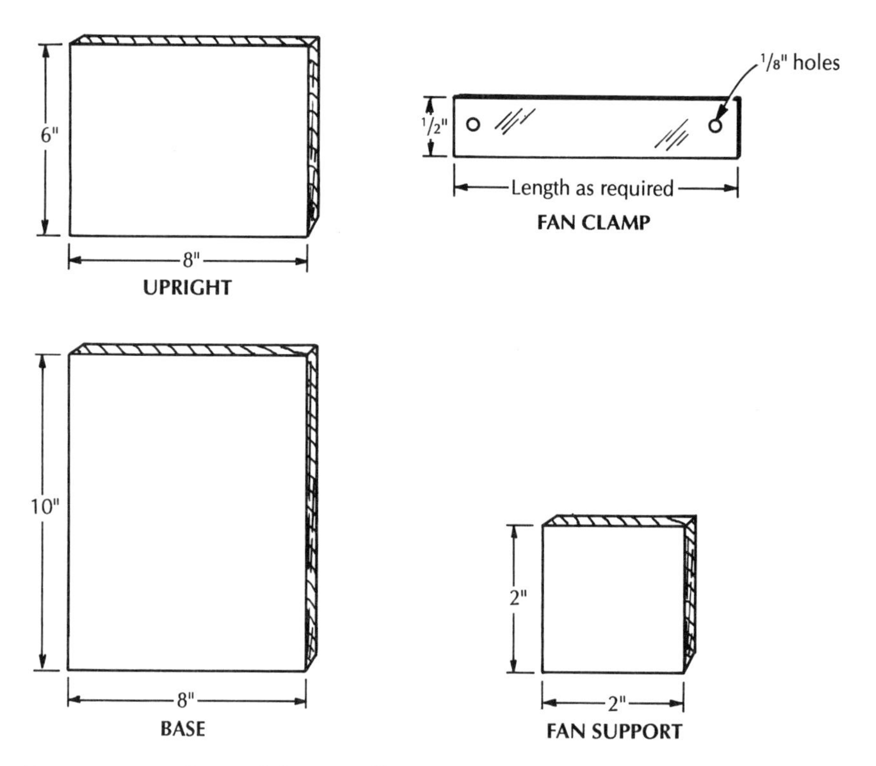

FIGURE 32 *Temperature-Control System Components*

FIGURE 33 *Complete Temperature-Control System*

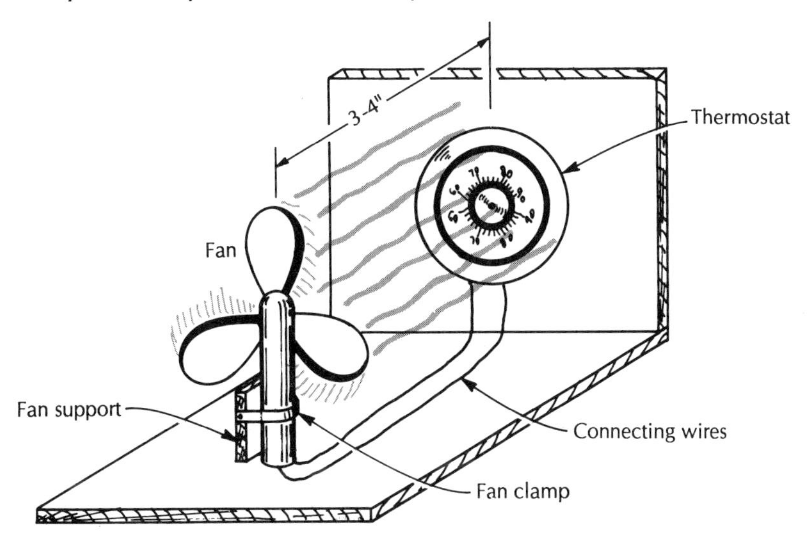

temperature of the room and opens or closes its contacts as a direct result of the rise and fall in temperature. The fan is the portion of the system that does the work. If the temperature is too high, the fan comes on and begins to cool—and continues to cool—the air until the temperature falls to the preselected level. When this level is reached, the thermostat turns off the fan and waits for the temperature to rise before turning it on again.

An argument could be made that this type of circuit exhibits rudimentary thought. If one considers the entire circuit as an entity, then the entity reacts to its surroundings by sensing temperature and taking steps to be sure that it does not overheat. Furthermore, it does this without anyone's intervention. In a similar fashion, our bodies also sense ambient temperature through sensors in our skin. If we get too hot, our bodies release liquid (perspiration) to cool us. Simple though it may be, the temperature-controlling circuit could easily be incorporated in a mechanical being.

The top and side views of another thinking machine are shown in Figure 34. This machine looks for a light source and then follows the

FIGURE 34 *Light Source Seeker*

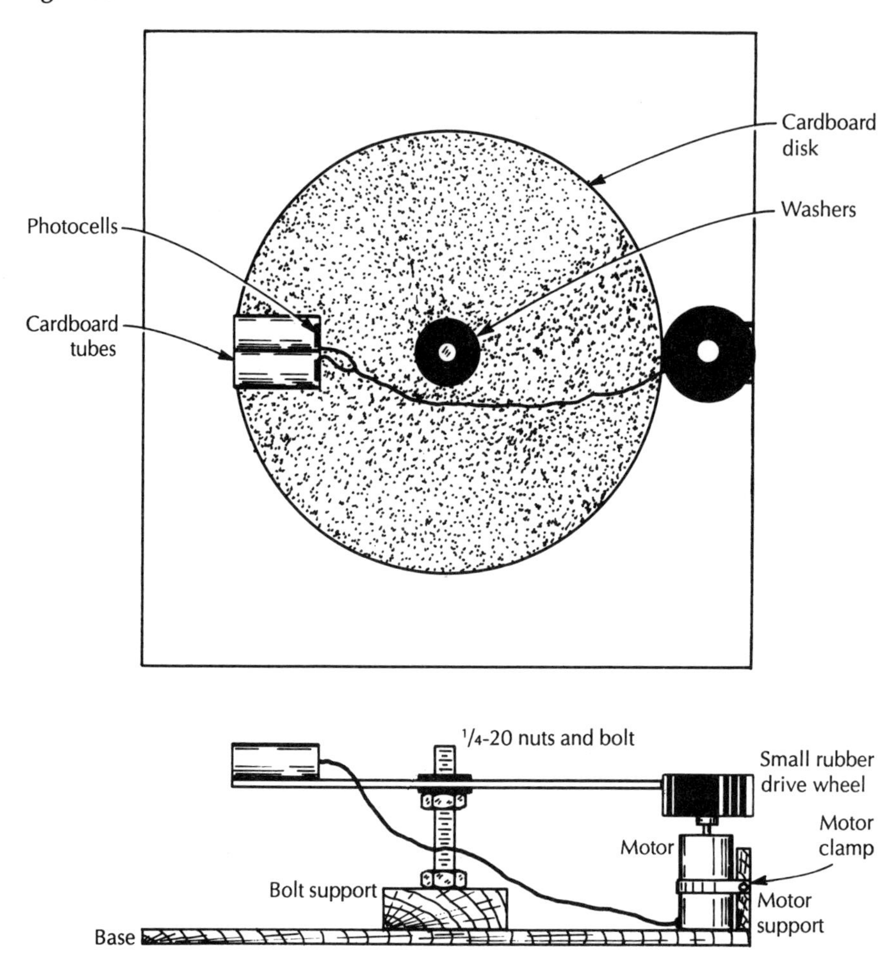

light as it moves. Such a machine might be used to track the sun during the day, always keeping a solar battery aligned on it for maximum energy. To build this device you will need two solar batteries, an inexpensive motor of the type that can be operated by the solar batteries, a few odds and ends, some scraps of wood, and some heavy cardboard, such as that backing an 8½ by 11-inch pad of paper. Referring to

FIGURE 35 *Main Cardboard Disk*

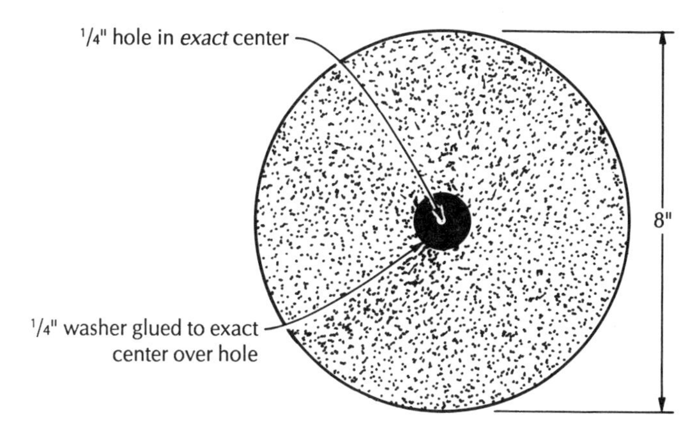

Figure 35, carefully cut the cardboard disk as close to a perfect circle as possible. Next glue two ¼-inch washers to the exact center of the disk, one on either side, to strengthen it, as shown. Use white glue or model airplane cement and allow it to fully dry. While the glue is drying, fabricate the wooden pieces and assemble the central shaft using a ¼-20, 3½-inch carriage bolt as shown in Figures 36 and 37. When this is completed, make the photocell sensors of cardboard and glue them to the disk as shown in Figure 38.

Carefully place the disk on the ¼-20 bolt and balance the disk with modeling clay until it sits level and turns freely. Then, clamp the motor to its support, position it, and arrange its shaft so that it touches and drives the disk on its edge. At this point you may wire the photocells, as shown in Figure 38, using thin-gauge wire to prevent excessive drag.

If the solar cells are aligned properly, and a strong beam of light is arranged to shine at the area just between them, the motor will turn the platform disk so that it faces directly into the beam of light. As you slowly move the light, the platform will attempt to follow.

Circuits such as the two described in this chapter are called servomechanisms in industry and are the basis of all thinking machines. These servomechanisms always contain sensors that check the environment and additional elements that do the actual work required. Automatic

FIGURE 36 *Seeker Components*

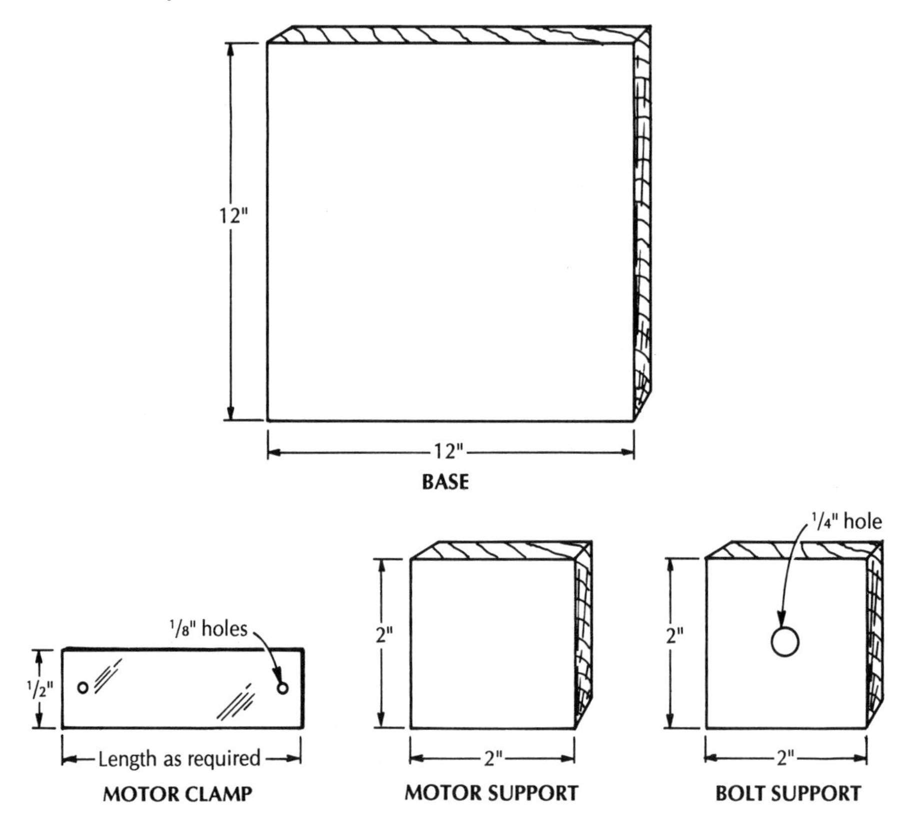

door openers, heating and air-conditioning systems, and even devices that turn on lights when it gets dark are all examples of servomechanisms. By understanding the circuits described in this chapter, you can

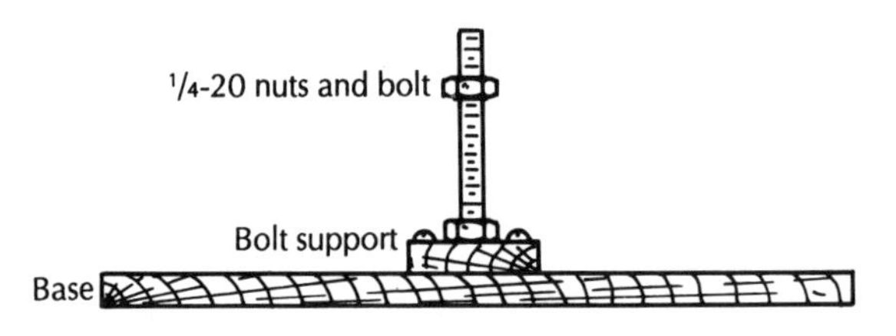

FIGURE 37 *Base and Main Disk Assembly*

FIGURE 38 *Photocell Assembly Details*

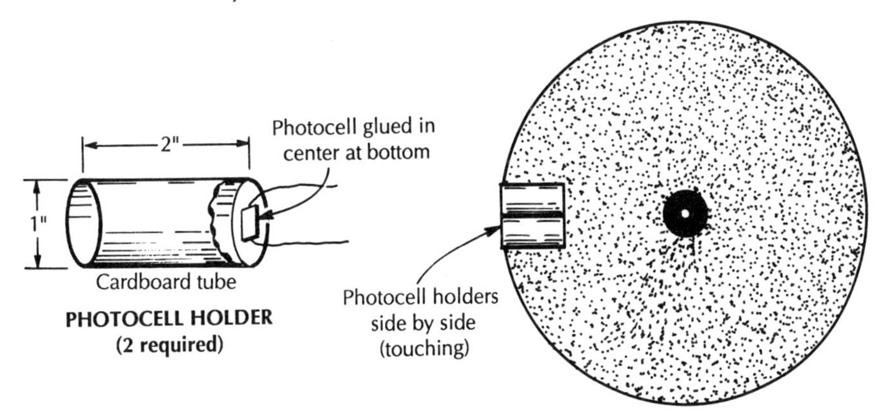

see how a robot might control its internal environment and how it might "see." Any future robot would, no doubt, contain thousands of servomechanisms of all sorts—much more sophisticated than the ones described here—to enable it to appear to be alive. It is interesting to contemplate whether such a device might be built so well that we would have trouble distinguishing it from a human being.

CHAPTER 7

Lasers

There are few basic technological developments that have captured the interest of the public to the extent that the laser has. Developed in 1960, the laser has found numerous applications in medicine, communications, manufacturing, and even weaponry of both the real world and the world of science fiction. There is no doubt that the laser is here to stay and will be an important part of the future.

Lasers have two features that make them unique and useful. The beam of light produced is unusually parallel and extremely pure. These features enable the laser device to have applications that are difficult, if not impossible, to achieve with any other light source.

There is a principle in optics that, in order to make a parallel, or collimated, beam of light, the source must be as small as possible. Figure 39 shows why this is so. An imaginary-point source, placed at the exact focal point of a lens, produces a perfectly parallel beam of light, as shown by the dotted lines. A real source, however, shown by the solid lines in the drawing, produces a spreading, or diverging, beam of light because it is larger than the focal point. Since the angle at which light is bent by the lens is constant at each point along the lens, light striking

FIGURE 39 *Comparison of Point Source and Real Source*

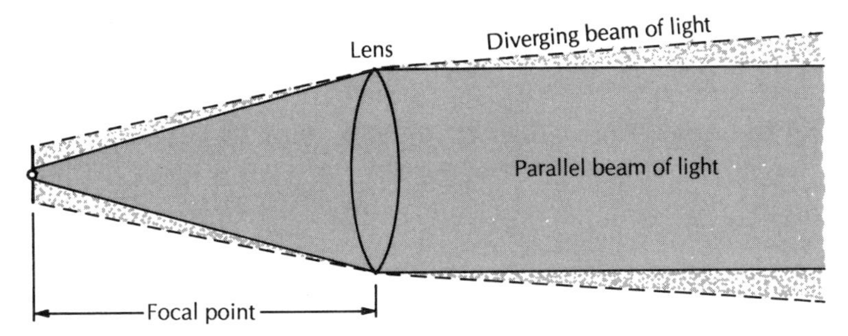

the lens from any point away from the exact focal point is bent away from parallel.

You can easily demonstrate this principle by obtaining a 2-inch to 3-inch diameter magnifying lens, a large and a small light source, and some simple materials. Referring to Figure 40, remove the shade from a table lamp so that the light bulb is in clear view. Turn on the lamp and move the lens between the bulb and a wall about 10 feet away until you see an image of the bulb on the wall. Now, have a friend move a piece of cardboard along the entire path from the lens to the wall and notice how the light spreads. By measuring the diameter of the bulb and its image on the far wall, you can determine the degree of divergence. Replace the lamp with a penlight and repeat the entire experiment. Notice how much less the divergence is. Finally, make the pinhole shown in Figure 41 by pushing a sewing needle through a piece of

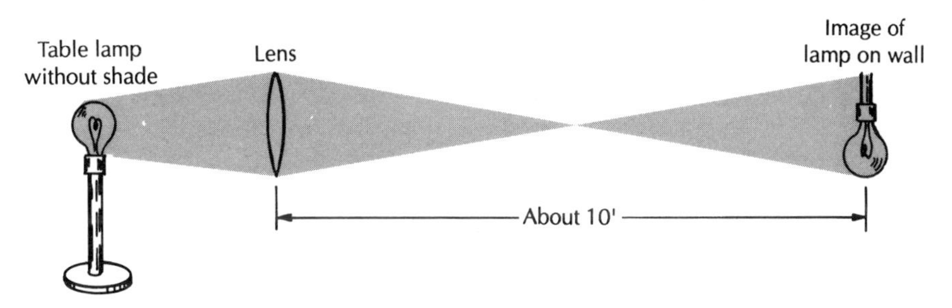

FIGURE 40 *Image of Lamp on Wall*

FIGURE 41 *Homemade Pinhole*

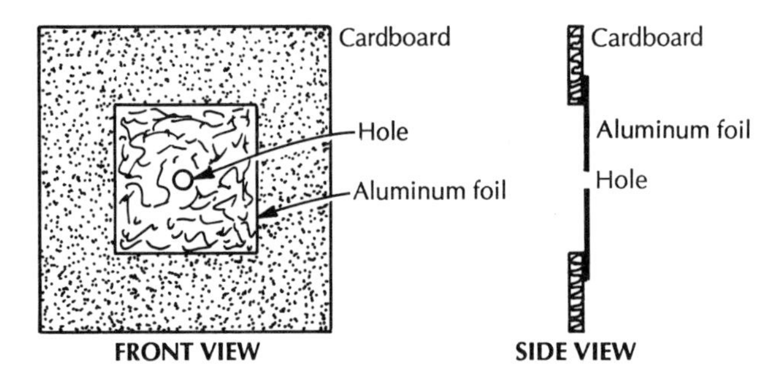

aluminum foil that has been pasted over a larger hole in a sheet of cardboard. Repeat the experiment, with the penlight illuminating the pinhole, as shown in Figure 42. You might have to darken the room to see the beam, but you will easily notice how superior the smaller source is to the two others.

A laser does not need pinholes. The simplest helium-neon devices produce intense beams of light that start out at about 1⁄32 of an inch in diameter and only diverge to 1⁄4 of an inch in diameter hundreds of feet away. The equivalent pinhole would have to be microscopic to accomplish the same results. Scientific-research lasers, fitted with external-lens assemblies, have produced beams of light that diverge so little that, when aimed at the moon (a distance of approximately 250,000 miles), the light beam is only 25 feet across when it reaches the moon!

The second feature of the laser is the purity of the light. We are all familiar with the color fringes that exist around bright objects viewed through a simple telescope or magnifying glass. These fringes occur

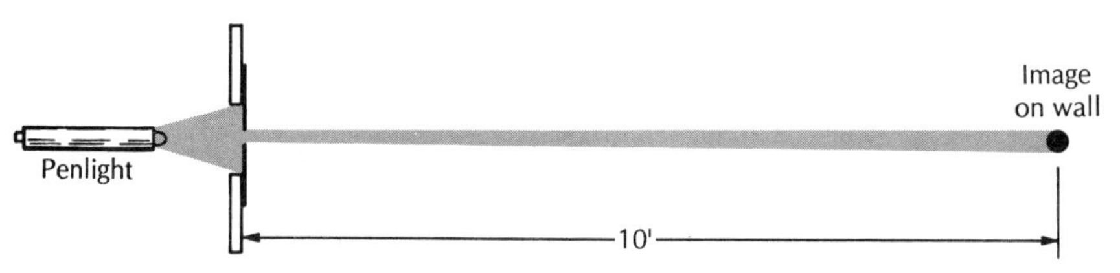

FIGURE 42 *Image of Penlight-Illuminated Pinhole on Wall*

FIGURE 43 *How White Light Is Focused with a Lens*

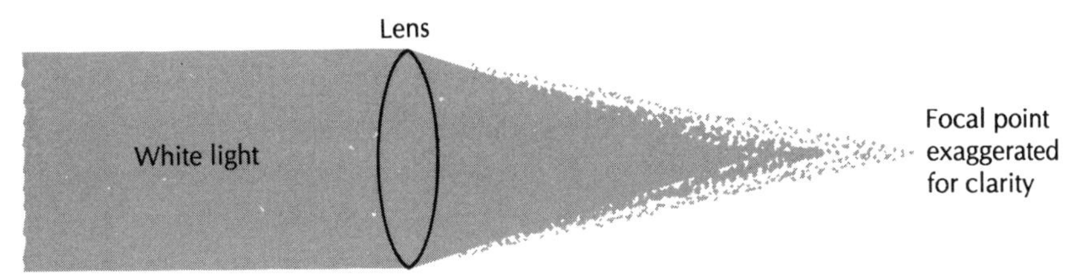

because a lens will bend light of different colors at different angles. Figure 43 shows how a white-light image is focused by a lens. You will notice that there is no clearly defined focal point, since each color focuses at a slightly different point.

A laser, on the other hand, only produces light of one color. This means that even a simple lens will focus all of a laser's light to a tiny point. This point can be so small, in fact, that it will fit within a single human cell. This means that a laser, producing a small amount of power, can be focused to a point that will get extremely hot—no energy being lost due to color-spreading and, thus, all energy being present within the point. In medical applications the temperatures reached are adequate to weld a detached retina in the eye or have the cutting ability to replace a scalpel in surgery. In industry special lasers can produce temperatures high enough to cut through steel plates. This is why it is so dangerous to stare directly into the output-beam of a laser. When focused onto the retina of the eye, the small intense spot of light produced by the lens of the eye can easily destroy individual cells causing partial, or even total, loss of sight.

If you take a magnifying glass outdoors on a sunny day and focus the image of the sun on a sheet of paper, as shown in Figure 44, the paper will darken and, eventually, begin to burn. This is with a light source 93,000,000 miles away and with a focused image only ⅛ inch across. Imagine the intense energy in a focused image 1/1,000 of an inch in diameter! If you do this experiment, be extremely careful. The paper can burst into flame very quickly.

FIGURE 44 *Effect of Concentrated Sunlight on Paper*

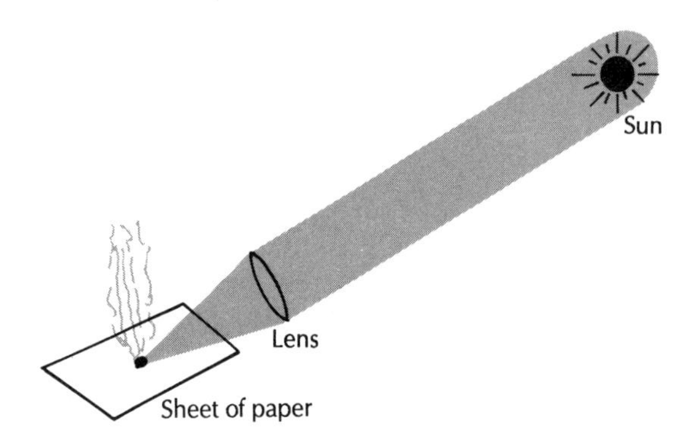

While the construction of an operating laser is beyond the scope of this book, a suitable substitute can be easily made. You will need a visible, high-output, light-emitting diode (LED); a small lens; a small on/off toggle switch; a 9-volt alkaline, transistor-radio battery; and a 330-ohm ¼-watt resistor. All of these parts can be obtained from a local electronics parts shop. For best results, choose an LED with a rated-power output of at least 2,000 mcd.

Begin construction by locating a cardboard tube that is slightly larger in inside diameter than the lens and about 3 inches longer than its focal length. The focal length of the lens is the distance from the surface of the lens to the focused image of the sun on the paper in the experiment of Figure 44. A tube such as the ones used for aluminum foil or paper towels is ideal if you can find a suitable lens. Otherwise, you will have to make a tube by rolling up some heavy paper. Referring

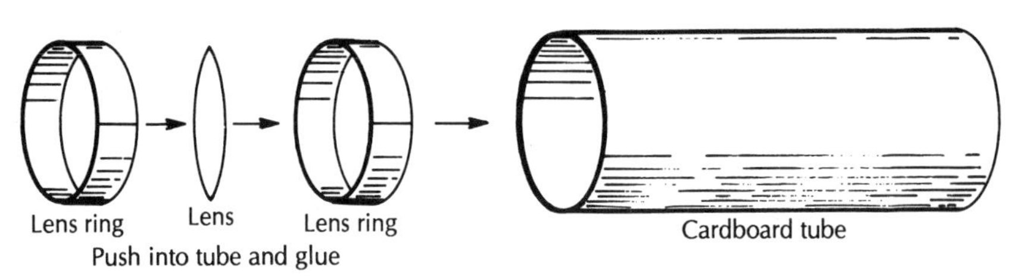

FIGURE 45 *Method of Mounting Lens*

FIGURE 46 *LED Holder*

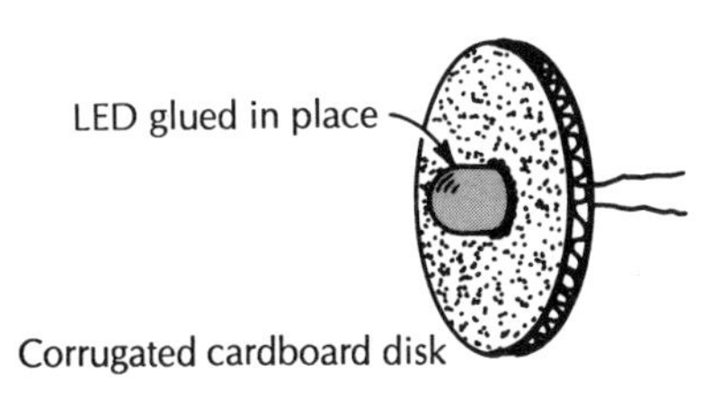

to Figure 45, cut two rings from one end of the tube and mount the lens, with white glue, at an end of the tube as shown. Next, from a corrugated, cardboard carton, cut a round disk of cardboard that will slide easily inside the tube. Punch a hole at the exact center of this disk with a pencil, push the LED through the hole, and glue it in place, as shown in Figure 46. Now slide the LED assembly into the open end of the tube and connect the battery, switch, and resistor. Figure 47 shows the final assembly. Turn on the switch and be sure that the LED lights. If it doesn't, check your connections and reverse the polarity of the battery. With the LED on, aim the lens at a distant wall, at least 10 feet or more away. Slowly slide the LED assembly back and forth until the smallest spot of light is produced on the wall. Glue the assembly in place, tucking the battery and resistor into the tube, and slide a corrugated, cardboard end-plate onto the end of the tube. This completes construction of the simulated laser, which, although not having anywhere near the power

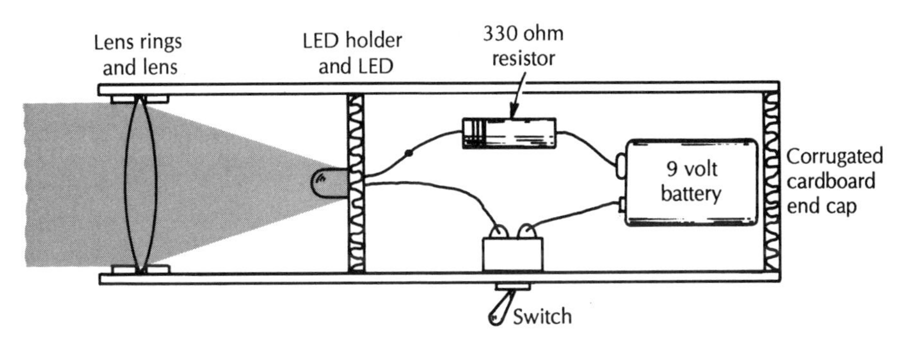

FIGURE 47 *Final Assembly of Simulated Laser*

or degree of parallelism in the output beam of a true laser, will serve as a safe, useful model of one.

In the future the parallelism aspect of the laser will be used in point-to-point free-air or free-space communications systems, in optical rulers or straightedges, in "pointers" for military weapons or industrial processes, and even in electro-optical fences and burglar alarms. The ability to produce high temperatures—due to the intense concentration of energy—will allow the development of exotic microsurgery, commercial cutting tools of all types, the transmission of power over long distances without the need for wires, and new generations of home-entertainment systems.

Magnetic Propulsion

Magnets, as we all know, come in many different sizes and shapes. They range from the tiny units found in toys and gadgets to giant electromagnets used to lift scrap metal and even whole automobiles in junkyards. We are also familiar with the most common physical property of magnets: Place two of them near each other, with the correct polarity on each, and they quickly jump together. Reverse the polarity of one, and they push each other apart, often with considerable force. It is precisely these features that may play a significant role in the technology of the future.

There are two basic types of magnets: the kind that are self-powered and the electromagnet. Self-powered magnets are called permanent magnets and are used in numerous devices from household appliances to scientific instruments. They are at the heart of most loudspeakers, small DC motors, phonographs, and tape recorder/players. Permanent magnets are naturally magnetic. They do not need any external power and can even be used to magnetize iron or steel rods simply by rubbing the rods along them. Electromagnets, on the other hand, require external power but are normally much more powerful—and they can be turned

FIGURE 48 *A Simple Electromagnet*

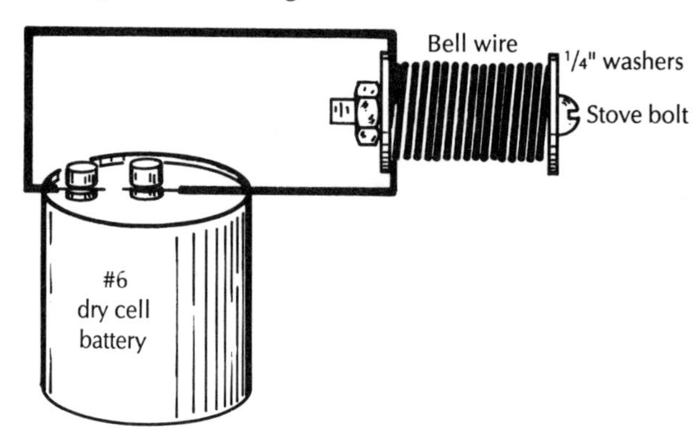

on and off. It is this latter characteristic that will be used in certain future technological developments.

We can build a simple electromagnet by winding 50 turns of bell wire around a ¼-inch by 3-inch iron stove bolt fitted with two ¼-inch flat washers and a nut as shown in Figure 48. Connect the ends of the wire winding to a #6 dry cell battery and note how the magnetic energy produced in the bolt picks up small nails, paper clips, pins, and so forth. Do not keep the magnet connected very long, however, as it draws appreciable power from the battery and will exhaust it if you allow the magnet to operate too long. If you were to increase the number of wire turns and the voltage, the magnet would get stronger. Commercial electromagnets have thousands of turns of wire and operate at power levels that are much higher than this model. Now, let us try something a little different.

Obtain a plastic soda straw, an iron or steel bolt that will just slide into the straw, and a push button switch, such as the one used to ring a doorbell. Be sure the bolt is magnetic by determining if it is attracted by a permanent magnet, and that it is at least 3 inches long. Cut the straw to a length of 4 inches, and then cut two 2-inch-diameter disks from cardboard and glue them to the straw, as shown in Figure 49. Now, carefully wind 100 turns of bell wire around the straw, between the disks, keeping each layer evenly spaced over the one below it. Do not crush the straw. Connect the coil, push button, and #6 dry cell battery,

FIGURE 49 *Straw Preparation*

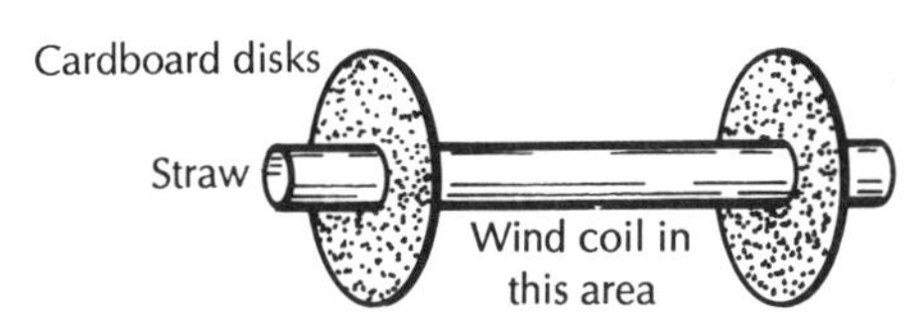

as shown in Figure 50, and place the bolt halfway into the straw. When you push the button, you will see that the bolt is quickly pulled into the coil. If you put a small pea, or similar object, in the straw prior to pushing the button, it will be expelled a considerable distance when the bolt is pulled in.

It is easy to visualize that a giant version of this simple device would make a powerful projectile launcher, or electromagnetic "gun." That is exactly what scientists at Sandia National Laboratories are proposing. Their application is not a weapon, however, but an alternative method of launching small satellites into earth orbit. Figure 51 shows the details of this system. A series of coils are arranged in a row to form the barrel of the launcher. An iron armature, with the satellite in a protective aeroshell, passes through the coils, reaching a velocity high enough to send the aeroshell above the main part of the earth's atmosphere. As the armature moves through each coil, sensors instruct a computer to turn on the power to the next coil at the correct instant to achieve

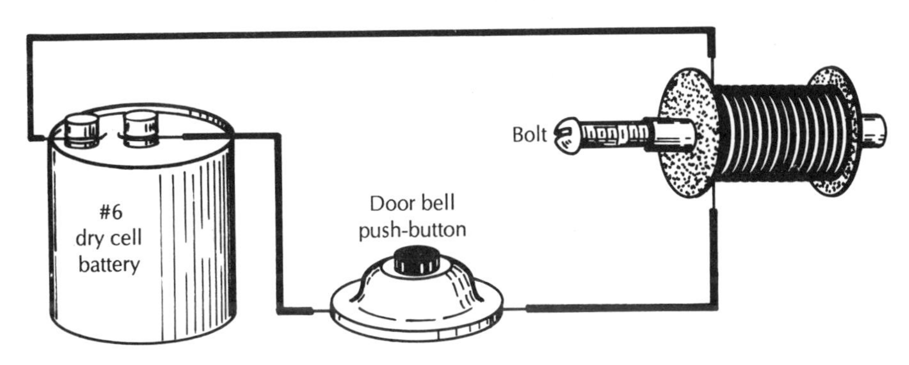

FIGURE 50 *Electromagnetic "Gun"*

FIGURE 51 *Proposed Satellite Launcher*

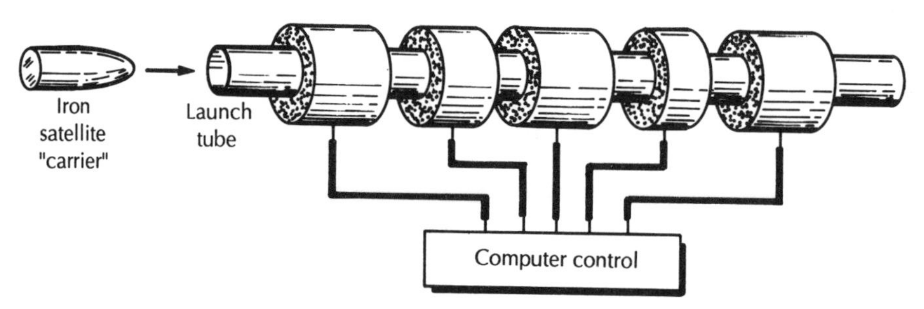

maximum thrust. Once the projectile is above the atmosphere, a small rocket motor is turned on to provide enough additional velocity to complete the trip into orbit. This combination of electromagnetic and rocket techniques would reduce costs and result in a much safer launch system.

Other scientists have proposed an earthbound high-speed travel system to replace conventional railroads, using a similar method, but without the rockets. Figure 52 shows this method, in which the electromagnetic coils are arranged along the route of the train and sequentially switched as it travels forward. By carefully controlling the power to each coil, the train can be made to accelerate, decelerate, travel at a constant speed, or stop.

Our electromagnetic model can be modified to demonstrate this

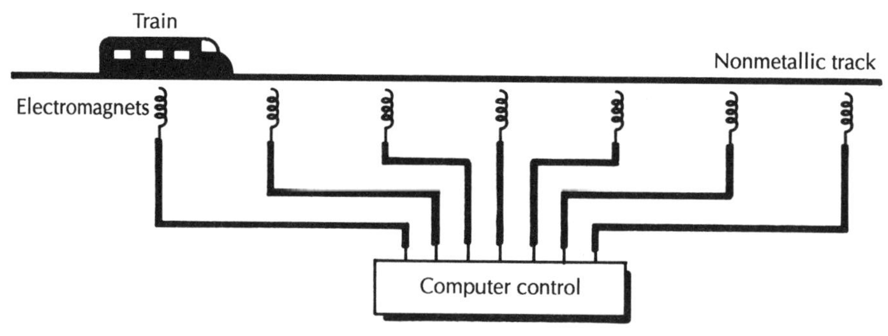

FIGURE 52 *Electromagnetic Train*

FIGURE 53 *Straw Preparation for Electromagnetic Train*

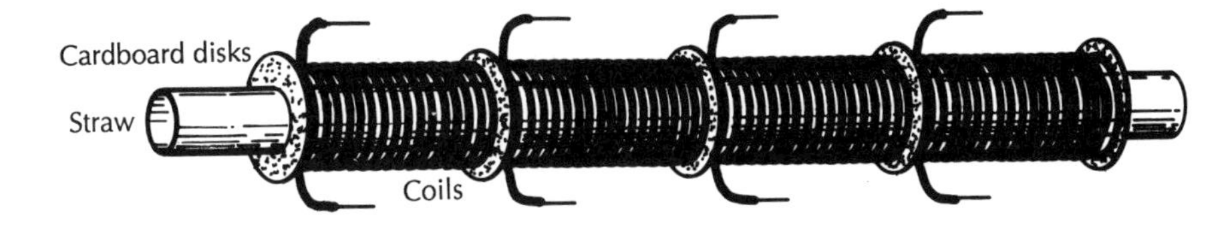

principle. Referring to Figure 53, cut five 2-inch-diameter cardboard disks and glue them to a new straw, as shown. Wind four 100-turn coils of bell wire—one between each of the disks. Now, referring to Figure 54, prepare the base and glue the coil assembly carefully to it. The coils should all have been wound in the same direction, and the bottom wire

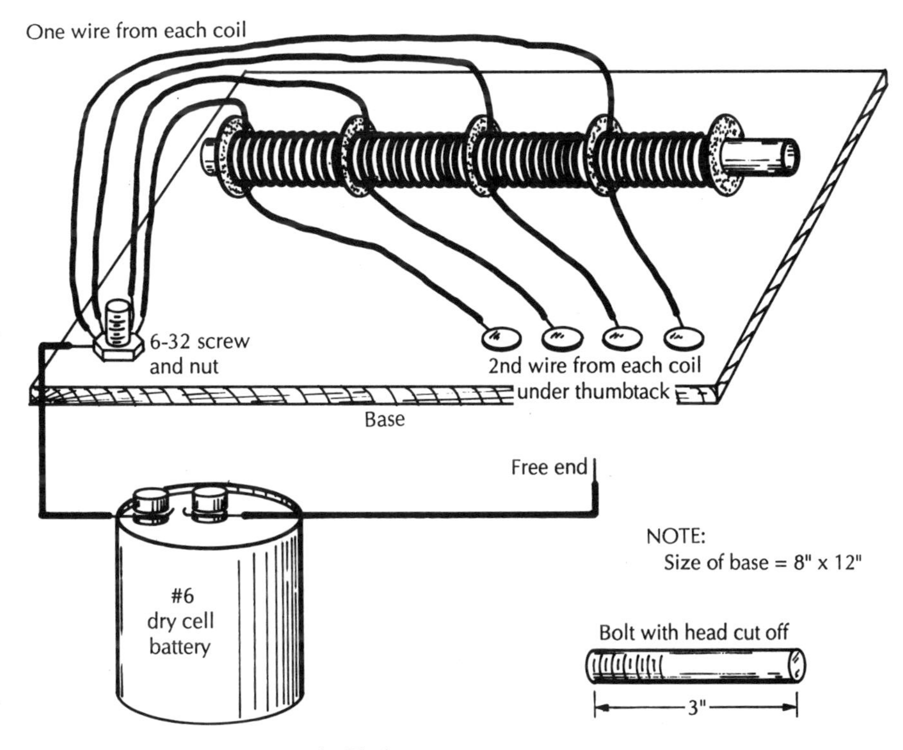

FIGURE 54 *Details of Electromagnetic Train*

from each coil should be connected to the 6-32 screw terminal. Be certain that the top wire from each coil makes good contact where it connects to the thumbtacks. Now, cut the head off a 3-inch bolt like the one used to make the electromagnet earlier in this chapter. Use a file to make certain the cut end is completely smooth and easily slides through the straw without binding. This bolt will represent one car of the train. Finally, connect the #6 dry cell battery to the assembly, and the railroad is ready for a trial run.

Place the bolt so that it is at one end of the straw and about halfway into the first coil. Slowly move the free end of the wire from the dry cell over the thumbtack contacts—one at a time, from left to right—and notice how the bolt moves through the straw. Repeat the process quickly and note that the bolt moves even more quickly and more smoothly. Move the wire from right to left over the contacts and the bolt will change direction. With a little practice, you will be able to get the bolt to travel through the entire straw quite rapidly in both directions.

To make magnetic propulsion systems such as these a reality on a practical scale requires large electromagnets, switching systems, and elaborate computer controls. These are all within the capabilities of today's technology, however, and could radically change the way we travel tomorrow.

Bioelectronics—"ESP, Telekinesis"

In the early 1900s, when the wonders of electricity were just beginning to be understood and appreciated, a number of experiments were conducted to see if many of the common human ailments could be cured by the application of electrical currents. While the results stated then seemed impressive, it seems that the only ones who truly benefited were the charlatans.

The medical profession uses all sorts of sophisticated electronics instruments today; and there is renewed interest in the direct application of minute electrical currents to the human body. Researchers have proven that, if properly applied and regulated, these currents do indeed speed up the healing of broken bones and torn ligaments and serve as an effective muscle relaxant for athletes. Future expansion of this technique may result in enabling broken bones to heal in only a day or so, as well as allowing deformed or even severed limbs to be, literally, regrown.

While it is too dangerous for the novice to experiment with such methods on himself, it is perfectly acceptable to do so on common plant life. If the experimental methods work on humans, it is certainly reasonable to think that they may also work, in a similar manner, on plants.

Figure 55 illustrates a wooden planting box that the experimenter can easily build to test the effects of electrical currents on plants. It is quite conventional, except for the sides and bottom. These are covered, in the interior, with thin aluminum plates, with contacts to terminals as shown. The aluminum is roof flashing, readily available at hardware stores. It is easily cut with a strong pair of scissors. When the box has been built, it should be filled with clean potting soil and some fast-germinating seeds, such as lima beans or peas, should be planted. The experimenter, under his own guidelines, should then apply a continuous electrical current between several plates, as desired, to see what happens. Experiments should be performed with both direct current, using a 6-volt lantern cell or a 1.5 volt #6 dry cell, and alternating current, using a simple 6- to 8-volt doorbell transformer obtained from a hard-

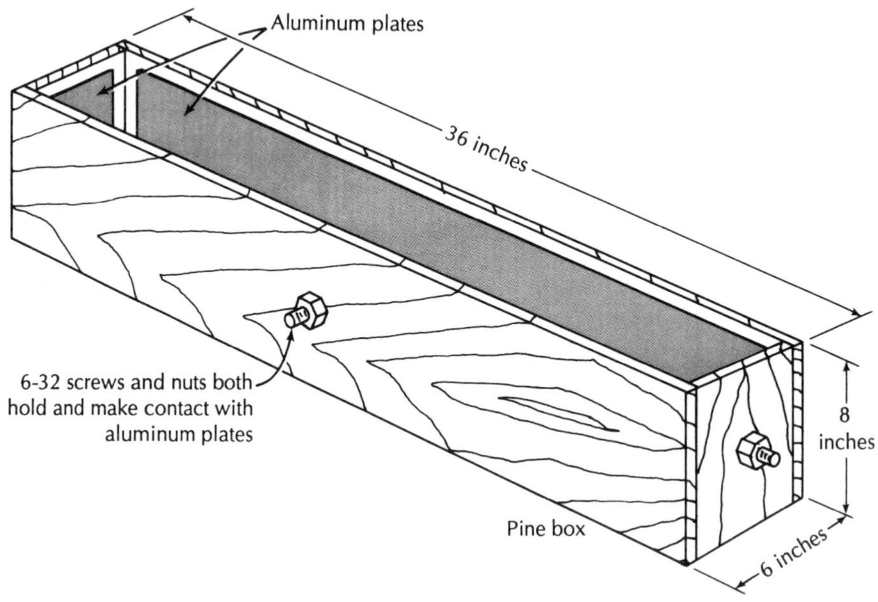

FIGURE 55 *Details of Planting Box*

FIGURE 56 *Method of Connecting a Low Voltage Transformer*

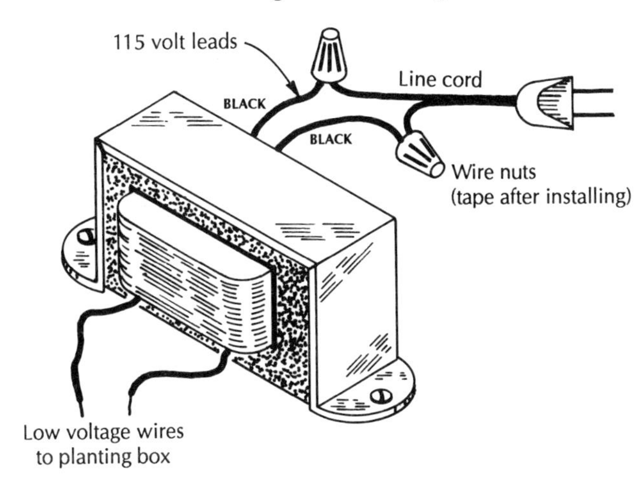

ware store. The way to make planter box connections to this transformer are given in Figure 56. When connecting the AC line cord to the transformer (the black wire), be absolutely certain that the connections are well insulated. After securely connecting the wires, thread wire nuts (also obtainable at a hardware store) over the twisted ends and then put black vinyl electrical tape over the wire nuts. The 115-volt pressure of the AC power line is quite high and can push enough current through a person to cause serious injury or, at least, a bad shock—so be very careful. The low voltage transformer output is quite safe, however. Although the drawing shows low voltage wires, some doorbell transformers are provided with screw terminals. If this is the case with the transformer you obtain, simply connect two lengths of wire to those terminals and you are ready for the experiment.

If the various experiments are performed carefully, and accurate records of results are kept, some new principle may be discovered. In doing these experiments, the plants should be watered regularly and subjected to the same care that is normally given to house plants. *For the source of current, only the AC or DC power sources described above should be used. NEVER CONNECT ANY EXPERIMENT DIRECTLY TO*

THE AC LINE. Furthermore, a 12-volt pilot lamp, obtained from an electronics parts distributor, should be connected, in series, with the power source. It is used to prevent overheating of the transformer if the two wires connected to the planting box accidentally touch each other. If results are obtained that seem interesting, the experiments should be repeated. For comparison, another planting box may be built and planted with the same kind of seeds as in the first box—but without using electrical current—as a way of testing the effect of the current.

In an even more interesting and unusual area, the experimenter can test the extrasensory perception (ESP) of various people as well as attempt to determine whether telekinesis, or "mind over matter," really exists. One should keep in mind that there are intelligent people who believe that there is more to these occult sciences than is apparent.

The ESP tester consists of a series of ten switches, arranged in two groups of five, as shown in Figure 57. The barrier blocks the transmitter's switches from being seen by the receiver. In operation, the transmitter closes a switch and projects his thoughts to the receiver. When the receiver thinks he knows which switch was closed, he activates his

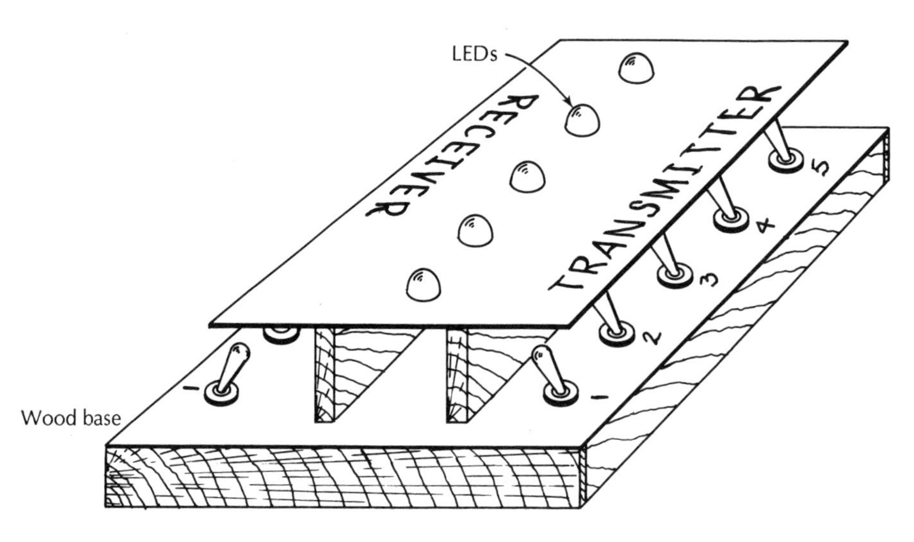

FIGURE 57 *Details of ESP Tester*

FIGURE 58 *Circuit of ESP Tester*

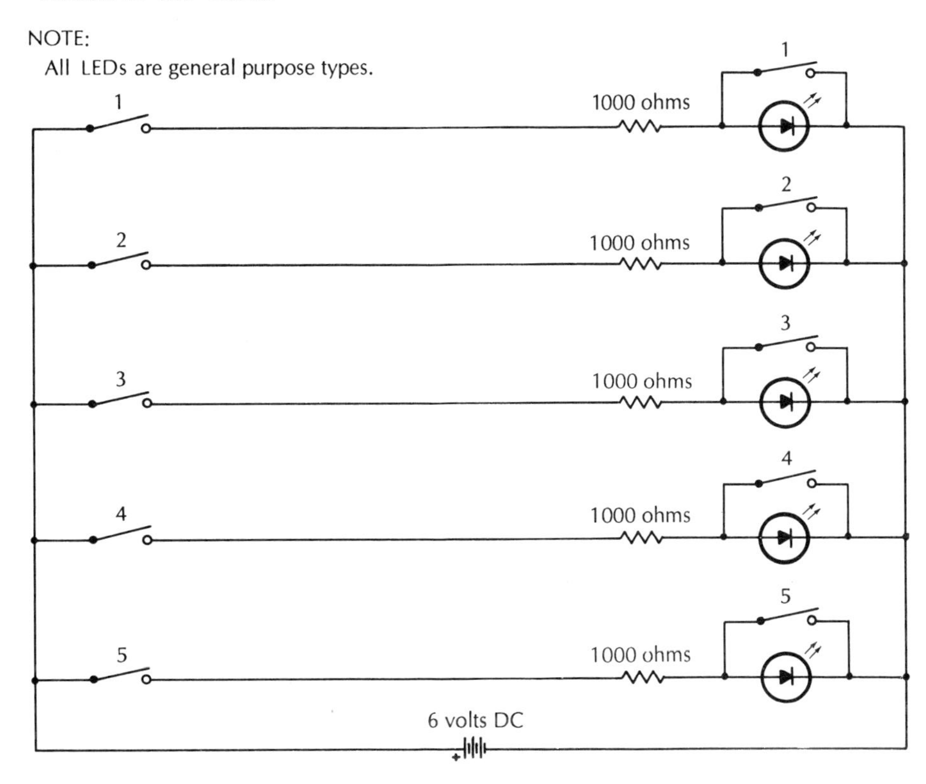

corresponding switch. A correct guess lights the LED associated with the switch. By keeping accurate records of 100 or more tries by various persons, the experimenter may be able to find someone with great ESP sensitivity, someone who does much better than the average person. The circuit of the ESP tester is shown in Figure 58. Note that the transmitter's switches are normally open and complete the circuit to one of the five LEDs. The receiver's switches are normally closed and short circuit the LEDs until opened. The 1,000-ohm resistors limit the battery current to the LEDs and prevent shorts. The switches are common SPST (single-pole, single-throw) toggle switches and the LEDs are inexpensive, general purpose indicators. A 6-volt lantern battery is used as a long-lasting source of power.

Testing "mind over matter" is a little more difficult. Any motion caused by a person as a result of thought is bound to be very small, so a sensitive motion detector is necessary. Figure 59 is such a unit. A brass weight is suspended on a fine wire in the center of a small nut. The system is then carefully adjusted so that the slightest movement causes the wire to contact the nut and thus, the circuit is completed. The wire is a single strand of common electrical zip cord and should be at least 3 to 4 feet long. The support should be as stable as possible and placed on the ground for even more stability. Finally, a plastic food container should be placed around the contacts to prevent air currents from trig-

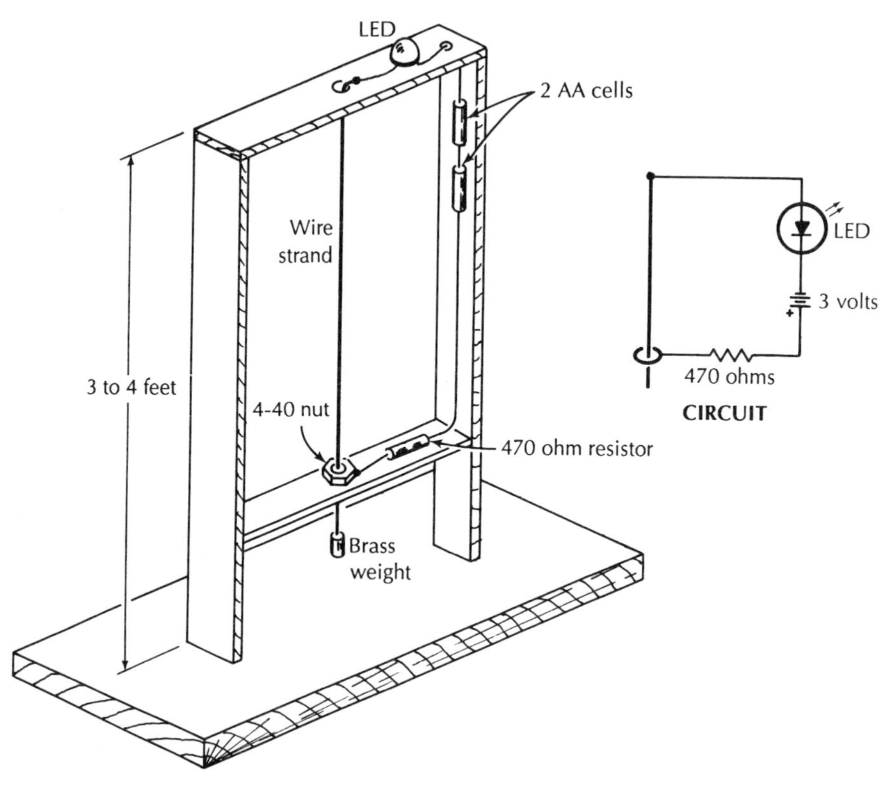

FIGURE 59 *Mind-Over-Matter Experiment*

gering the circuit. At this point, various people should be encouraged to attempt to complete the circuit with their thoughts.

It should be most interesting to see if any of these way-out investigations develops into anything more concrete in years to come.

CHAPTER 10

Computers

The modern computer, using integrated circuits (silicon chips) containing, literally, tens of thousands of transistors and other electronic components that are connected in complex configurations, does all sorts of computations, record keeping, and even game playing. What it does not do, even though at times it certainly seems to do so, is think. It is only capable of following the instructions of a clever program that has been prepared for it. This task, however, it performs flawlessly.

The computer of the future will have to do more. As its uses become even more widespread, it will have to interact directly with ordinary people, not trained programmers or data-entry personnel. It will have to react in ways that will enable it to learn from its own mistakes and from the mistakes of the people it deals with. This will require that the computer possess some form of artificial intelligence as well as simple, easy-to-understand, interface programming.

In this chapter we will examine two authentic computer programs that can be used by the experimenter to gain an insight into man/machine interfaces, as well as intelligent conversation with a machine. A true artificial-intelligence program is beyond the scope of this book, but the examples that follow should give you a clear idea of what the

FIGURE 60 *Introductory BASIC Computer Program*

```
10 CLS
20 INPUT "WHAT IS YOUR NAME";A$
30 PRINT
40 PRINT "HELLO "A$
50 PRINT
60 PRINT "IS THERE ANYONE ELSE I SHOULD KNOW?"
70 INPUT "(PLEASE ANSWER YES OR NO)";B$
80 IF B$ <> "YES" GOTO 150
90 PRINT
100 INPUT "WHAT IS THEIR NAME";B$
110 PRINT
120 PRINT "HELLO "B$
130 PRINT
140 GOTO 60
150 PRINT
160 PRINT "IT WAS NICE MEETING YOU "A$
170 PRINT
180 PRINT "HAVE A NICE DAY"
190 END
0
```

programmers are working on. Both programs are written in a language called BASIC and can be used on any computer that is set up to operate in any of the various forms of this language.

The first program is shown in Figure 60. It is very elementary, but does show how a computer program can easily interact with a person. The number to the left of each statement indicates the order in which the computer will look at each line. Normally, space is left between the lines for the insertion of additional statements as the program is modified. That is why the lines are numbered in steps of ten. You could add a line between 10 and 20, for example, by calling it 15. The operation of this program is as follows:

> Line 10 sets the stage by telling the computer to clear the screen of any writing to avoid confusion.
>
> Line 20 tells the computer to print the statement "What is your name?" and then to wait for an answer (input) that it will recognize as A$. When a name is typed on the computer's keyboard, all of the characters of that name will be stored as the symbol A$ in the computer's memory.

Line 30 tells the computer to print nothing on the screen, which it interprets as "skip a line."

Line 40 is the computer's first answer. As you can see, it will print "Hello" followed by whatever is stored as A$.

Line 50 again skips a line.

Lines 60 and 70 tell the computer to print "Is there anyone else I should know?" and, then, to wait for an input, which should be "yes" or "no." The computer will store this input as B$.

Line 80 tells the computer to make a decision based upon the response to the question posed in line 60. If B$ is not equal to a "yes" answer, the computer must jump to the instructions in line 150. Otherwise it continues to line 90.

Lines 90 through 130 are similar to lines 20 through 50 and ask similar questions.

Line 140 tells the computer to go back to line 60, forming a loop that will continue indefinitely until the response to the question in line 70 is "no."

Lines 150 through the end, line 190, present the closing statements of the program.

When typing this program into a computer, you should be careful to copy each line exactly as shown for the proper results. Remember, the computer cannot possibly know what you really mean, it can only respond to precisely what you have entered. If you spell anything incorrectly or leave out the space between the letter O and the quotation marks in lines 40 and 50, or between the letter U and the quotation marks in line 160, the program will not give the proper results.

Once you have entered the program and rechecked that all lines have been entered exactly as shown, type the word *RUN* and the computer will execute the program. If you use your imagination, within the limits of this simple program, you will realize that you are really carrying on a conversation with the computer. It is the sophisticated extensions of such programs that will be the input mechanism of future machines.

The program in Figure 61 is a bit more elaborate. It is a computerized variation of the common guess-the-number-I-am-thinking-of game

```
10 CLS
20 PRINT"HELLO, I WOULD LIKE TO SHOW YOU HOW SMART I AM SO LET'S PLAY A GAME"
30 PRINT
40 PRINT"YOU CHOOSE A NUMBER AND I WILL TRY TO GUESS IT"
50 PRINT
60 PRINT"SINCE I AM ONLY A COMPUTER AND NOT A MIND READER"
70 PRINT"THERE HAVE TO BE CERTAIN LIMITS. SO:"
80 PRINT
90 PRINT"THE NUMBER YOU CHOOSE MUST BE BETWEEN 0 AND 100"
100 PRINT
110 PRINT"THE NUMBER MUST BE A WHOLE NUMBER"
120 PRINT
130 PRINT"ENTER 'H' IF MY GUESS IS TOO HIGH"
140 PRINT"ENTER 'L' IF MY GUESS IS TOO LOW"
150 PRINT"ENTER 'OK' IF MY GUESS IS CORRECT"
160 PRINT
170 PRINT"NOW CHOOSE THE NUMBER BUT DON'T TELL ME"
180 PRINT
190 INPUT"DO YOU HAVE YOUR NUMBER (Y OR N)";Q$
200 IF Q$<>"Y" THEN PRINT:GOTO 190
210 L=1:H=100:T=0
220 IF L>H GOTO 340
230 X=INT((L+H)/2)
240 CLS
250 PRINT"LET ME SEE, HMMM, I THINK I WILL GUESS"
260 PRINT
270 PRINT X
280 PRINT
290 INPUT"AM I TOO HIGH (H), TOO LOW (L), OR DID I GET IT (OK)";A$
300 T=T+1
310 IF A$="H" THEN H=X-1:GOTO 220
320 IF A$="L" THEN L=X+1:GOTO 220
330 IF A$="OK" THEN GOTO 380
340 PRINT
350 PRINT"I THINK YOU ARE FOOLING ME, LET'S TRY AGAIN"
360 PRINT
370 INPUT"AND THIS TIME, GIVE ME THE RIGHT ANSWERS, OK";Q$:GOTO 180
380 CLS
390 PRINT
400 PRINT"HOORAY I GOT IT!!"
410 PRINT
420 PRINT"AND IT ONLY TOOK ";T;" TURNS"
430 PRINT
440 PRINT"NOT BAD FOR A MACHINE!!"
450 PRINT:PRINT:PRINT
460 INPUT"DO YOU WISH TO TEST MY INTELLIGENCE AGAIN (Y OR N)";Q$
470 IF Q$<>"Y" GOTO 500
480 GOTO 180
490 PRINT
500 PRINT"THANKS FOR INTERACTING WITH ME. I HOPE YOU ENJOYED IT":END
```

FIGURE 61 *Human/Computer Interface Program*

children often play, except this time it is the computer that is doing the guessing. When playing this game with the computer it does seem that the computer is intelligent, but, if you examine the BASIC program statements, you will see that, again, the computer is only doing what it has been told to do.

Lines 10 through 180 are simply statements that tell the player what the rules are.

Line 210 sets the limits of the game between 1 and 100.

Line 230 tells the computer to guess halfway between the two limits, which will change as the guessing progresses. The "INT" statement rounds off the number so that fractions do not occur.

Lines 310 and 320 narrow the range of guesses until the actual number is finally arrived at.

When typing this program into a computer, as in the case of the first program, be careful to copy each line exactly as shown for the proper results. Remember, the computer can only respond to precisely what you have entered. Once you have entered the program and re-checked that all lines have been entered exactly as shown, type the word *RUN* and the computer will execute the program.

INDEX